"What the hell do you think you're doing here?"

Andrea gripped her shoulder bag tightly and faced Kane Mallory head-on. "I've come to get Kip."

"So! You're the kid sister? What was the plan, to construct a litter and drag him back through the jungle?"

He sounded so scathing that Andrea glared at him. *She* was the one with reason to be scathing. This was the man who had sent half a telephone message and nothing more, she was quite sure of that. Everything about him said that he wouldn't be bothered to act in any kindly manner.

"Very haughty," he observed sarcastically, his dark brows meeting in a scowl. "Your brother has flown out from Nairobi two days ago; by now he will be tucked up in hospital in London at the company's expense. Because there's nobody, apparently, to curb your juvenile enthusiasms when Kip is away, I now have you on my hands!"

PATRICIA WILSON used to live in Yorkshire, England, but with her children all grown up, she decided to give up her teaching position there and accompany her husband on an extended trip to Spain. Their travels are providing her with plenty of inspiration for her romance writing.

Don't miss Patricia Wilson's new Madembi romance, *Jungle Enchantment,* available in June from Harlequin Presents. Andrea's brother, Kip, will finally meet his match!

Books by Patricia Wilson

HARLEQUIN PRESENTS
1310—A SECRET UNDERSTANDING
1398—PASSIONATE ENEMY
1430—STORMY SURRENDER
1454—CURTAIN OF STARS
1469—THE GIFT OF LOVING
1518—PERILOUS REFUGE

HARLEQUIN ROMANCE
2856—BRIDE OF DIAZ
3102—BOND OF DESTINY

PATRICIA WILSON

Forbidden Enchantment

Harlequin Books

TORONTO • NEW YORK • LONDON
AMSTERDAM • PARIS • SYDNEY • HAMBURG
STOCKHOLM • ATHENS • TOKYO • MILAN
MADRID • WARSAW • BUDAPEST • AUCKLAND

Harlequin Presents first edition April 1993
ISBN 0-373-11547-4

Original hardcover edition published in 1991
by Mills & Boon Limited

FORBIDDEN ENCHANTMENT

CHAPTER ONE

'AFRICA! Andrea, you can't! I told you what would happen when Kip went out there. Now look! It's *happened*!'

Andrea Forsythe regarded her Aunt Maureen sternly.

'Africa is not the end of the world. I'm going by air, not by dug-out canoe, and, as for Kip, he could have had an accident anywhere. It's a dangerous job whether he does it in Africa or Brighton.'

'They don't build dams in Brighton.' Aunt Maureen sniffed. 'He's out there all alone, probably crippled.'

Hysteria seemed to be threatening again and Andrea had to take a firm grip on the situation before her aunt spun out of control.

'He won't be all alone because I'm going out to get him,' she pointed out doggedly. 'That garbled message we had just won't do. You'd think that a firm as big as Mallory-Carter could take more care of their employees and get some sort of comforting news to relatives when anything goes wrong. It's diabolical!'

'Maybe the dam burst!'

Maureen Forsythe's blood-curdling whisper was just about the last straw and Andrea sat at the table opposite ready to read the Riot Act before her aunt crumbled completely. She often wondered who had brought whom up! Her father's delicate-looking sister had reared both herself and Kip since they were children but it was Kip who had planned things, Andrea who had backed him to the hilt, both of them keeping an affectionate eye on their sensitive guardian, guiding her along the path of unexpected responsibility.

'The dam isn't built yet, so it can hardly burst. Now do let's be sensible, Aunt Maureen. Kip has had an accident. We got a brief phone call that was mysteriously cut off and then nothing, no letter, no cable, nothing! I'm going out to Madembi to find out where Kip is and I'm bringing him back. If Mallory-Carter can't cope, I *will*!'

'You were always headstrong, dear,' Aunt Maureen murmured, eyeing Andrea with a certain amount of apprehension. 'You're very small, though.'

'Petite,' Andrea pointed out serenely. 'Small of frame and tough of nature. I'm not going to try to carry Kip back. I'll see how he is and get him on a plane and I'll give them a piece of my mind while I'm about it too. They needn't think they can get away with this sort of conduct. The next victim may not have a relative handy to take charge.'

'Oh, I don't think they'll let you take charge, dear. In any case, you're studying for your doctorate,' her aunt reminded her with shaky triumph.

'Not all through the long vac, darling. Now no more hedging. Don't you want to see Kip safe and sound, back at home?' Andrea allowed a small amount of cajoling to enter her tone, a sure-fire way of getting round Aunt Maureen's anxieties.

'Of course I do, Andrea! I'm going out of my mind but I might lose you too...' Her voice trailed away miserably and Andrea patted her hand and then stood up with a 'no more nonsense' look on her face.

'It's impossible to lose me. Many have tried but none have succeeded. One week and I'll have Kip here and tucked up in bed.'

Her aunt conceded, tearfully. She knew it was also impossible to divert Andrea when her mind was made up and she knew too that Kip and Andrea were closer than most brothers and sisters. They had lost their parents at such a vulnerable age. Looking after them had been a delight even though the circumstances were tragic: a road accident, her brother and his wife so young, Andrea and Kip left alone.

Andrea had been so tiny at eight years old, doll-like and beautiful. Kip, at twelve, had already developed a strongly protective attitude when it came to his small, delicate-looking sister but Maureen had soon found out that Andrea's delicate beauty and tiny size were deceptive. She could take care of herself and fought like a tiger if Kip was in any trouble. What could she expect now but that Andrea would go rushing out to see what was happening?

'All right, dear,' she sighed. 'Just take care, though.'

'Don't worry.' Andrea bent her astonishingly fair head and rubbed her cheek affectionately against her aunt's. 'I'm bigger than I look. It's somebody at Mallory-Carter who'll have to look out. I expect the site manager or some such body has made a hash of things. Kip's probably in some awful African hospital. I bet they haven't even flown him out to Nairobi!'

'Oh, darling!' Aunt Maureen looked pale and Andrea regretted voicing her darkest suspicions.

'I'll see to it,' she emphasised crisply. 'Don't worry!'

Andrea *was* worried, though. She flew out next day, having been lucky enough to get a flight to Nairobi and a vague promise of a connecting flight to Madembi. She had been told that she would probably get one when she reached Kenya and it was that 'probably' that still rang ominously in her mind. Kip just couldn't be left alone and she was having terrible thoughts of the condition he would be in. They just didn't *know*! That was the worst thing—not knowing. If anything happened to Kip...

He was twenty-eight, four years older than she was, and he had always been her helper, her protector. She adored Kip. She had been as scared as Aunt Maureen when he had gone out to Africa as one of the engineers on the giant Kabala Dam in the young state of Madembi, but she would never have voiced her fears. Kip had wanted to go, had been excited, and to try to stop him with female tears would have been wicked in Andrea's opinion.

She settled back in her seat. Soon they would be dimming the lights for sleep but she had never felt so far away from sleep. The steward looked at her admiringly as he passed.

'A drink before we settle for the night, miss?'

Andrea shook her fair head and smiled. She didn't know what sort of a drink he was offering but she would need all her wits about her tomorrow and she wasn't used to drinking at all.

She was slight, willowy, her finely boned face dominated by wide tilting eyes of dark brown, a startling contrast with hair that was a true ash blonde. Her hair fell in soft, silky waves to her shoulders, framing a beautiful face. She was not exactly tiny but her delicate bones, her five-foot-two height and her innocent face brought out the protector in most males, the wolf in others. The wolves she dispatched with a ready tongue and an icy look. She usually ended up protecting the would-be protectors. She felt protective about Kip even though he was older. Maybe it was because even at eight she had sensed Aunt Maureen's inability to cope thoroughly and had realised that, young as they were, she and Kip had also taken on a responsibility.

The handsome cottage in Derbyshire had been a happy home, though, and now she was at Oxford, working for her Ph.D. in History. The thought brought Kip back to her mind. It was Kip who had persuaded her to continue and it was Kip's generosity that had made it possible for her to have her own flat in Oxford.

'I'm making plenty, kiddo,' he had said with a laugh when she had protested. 'Can't have you up half the night listening to somebody else's pop music.'

'Does that mean I have to keep my nose to the grind-stone?' she had asked mockingly.

'Is it likely with a face like that?' Kip had enquired with smiling irony. 'I know about the steady stream of admirers. I just want you to have the choice to go out or stay in, that's all.'

'I've got a grant,' Andrea had reminded him.

'And I've got a job that pays a bomb. Besides, what am I going to spend it on in Madembi? Let me help, love.'

Now she had to help Kip because somewhere out there he was hurt, injured. In front of Aunt Maureen she had kept a stiff upper lip, but now her imagination ran riot. He had worked as an engineer for Mallory-Carter, the giant Canadian firm, ever since he left university. They built dams and irrigation projects all over the world and she had assumed that with such a giant firm he would be safe.

Apparently, though, you were only all right with them if you kept on your feet! There had been a phone call one day to Aunt Maureen. Kip had been injured. It had been cut off before any more details were given and whoever had rung had not tried again. Maybe it was a hoax? Andrea bit her soft lower lip and shook her head. Unlikely. It wasn't the sort of thing to amuse anyone who worked on dams. It was dangerous enough as it was and nobody else would have had her aunt's telephone number. No, it had to be someone in authority—the site manager most likely.

She already had a vivid mental image of *him*! He would be grizzled and rough, burned by the sun like old leather, a bully who didn't care two hoots for people's feelings. She knew what she would be facing.

'Tea, Miss Forsythe?' Andrea opened her eyes in surprise to find that she had slept after all and the steward was bending over her solicitously. The lights were off now altogether and red sunlight filtered into the air-conditioned cabin of the big jet.

'Thank you.' Her eyes slid to the window and he smiled knowingly.

'Sunrise over the Sahara. A romantic sight.'

She would have agreed except that there was no sign of the Sahara, as they were too high, and a red sunrise was a red sunrise wherever it was. She smiled brightly and drank her tea and he departed with a smug smile. He had engaged that beautiful little thing in conversation. He didn't usually bother but in this case he was prepared to make an exception. She seemed to have stepped right out of a picture book. He assumed, erroneously, that she needed looking after. Pity that he wouldn't have the chance.

Getting to Madembi proved to be a problem and it was the next day before Andrea managed to get a flight. Apparently there were few flights in and the day's flight had gone before she had landed from London. It was time-consuming, tiresome and only increased her anxiety.

It was lunchtime next day before she actually arrived there, thankful as it turned out that there had been a meal of sorts on the flight because when she saw the airport in Madembi—the only airport—she knew she would never have been able to eat here, even if she had wanted to.

There was a tight, hostile feeling about the place, an air of waiting, and few people about, considering that this airport dealt with flights from all over Africa. Most of the people at the airport seemed to be soldiers, their olive-green uniforms somehow frightening. Those who noticed her stared at her disapprovingly, the disapproval mainly directed at her short denim skirt and the length of her legs. She wished now that she had worn trousers, but it was so *hot*!

Even trousers would have been out of place, she realised as she saw a few women. They were in long dresses that trailed on the dusty road, their sleeves short and full like those of women from some Victorian missionary school. She amused them, apparently, because they looked her over and giggled loudly, nudging each other. It wouldn't have done anything for her self-confidence if it had needed a boost. Fortunately, it didn't need anything of the sort. She was always perfectly sure of herself and on this occasion she was on a mission that was particularly close to her heart. Nothing was going to sidetrack her.

The soldiers looked on grimly and nobody spoke to her at all. She showed her passport at the flimsy desk that dealt with such things and asked about getting to the Kabala Dam, and it stunned her to discover that she was being totally ignored. She might as well have been from Mars. Nobody took any notice of her. They conversed together as if she was not there and had never spoken at all. The man at the desk returned her passport, pursed his lips disapprovingly and waved her on.

'How do I...?'

He began to deal with the next person as if Andrea was invisible and two soldiers wandered over to watch her grimly. She decided to get out of there fast without drawing any further attention to herself. Something was definitely wrong, even taking into account her short skirt. If Kip was stranded here without medical aid she could imagine his state of distress.

Even though she was furious she felt a bit shaky inside and it suddenly occurred to her that she was more than a little scared. The whole atmosphere was just that bit sinister—more than a bit—and she left the building rapidly, grabbing her travelling bag and walking swiftly away, her temper beginning to rise further as she realised that this was almost like running away at the first sign of trouble.

There were no taxis. The airport was well outside the nearest town. She couldn't even remember the name of the town anyway. Kip had written about it with some enthusiasm but she was in too much of a state right now to even think straight. She seemed to be on a dusty deserted street with quite a few menacing soldiers in the airport building ready to take her to task if she went back inside and demanded help.

It was searingly hot, still and humid and perspiration was already beginning to make her feel uncomfortable. The dust seemed to be rising with the heat and there was a threatening, unnatural silence. This place should have been busy. There had been freight on the plane. She had seen them loading it at Nairobi. Where *was* everybody?

She sat on a dirty-looking bench and looked around, listening to the almost uncanny stillness as her eyes took in the scene. There was no visible township. After the wide avenues and tall buildings of Nairobi this seemed to be the end of the earth.

The land around the airport had been cleared at some time past and now was little more than scrubland—bush. A few trees still flourished, impossibly verdant in a dusty landscape, but not too far away she could see that the red dusty track led into wilder land where the trees grew tall and reached for the sunlight, the dark green belt looking impenetrable except for the wide track that bore the marks of heavy lorries, the caterpillar tracks of heavy equipment, the weight of them having beaten down the dust and making a red earthen path that was wide and clear. She almost shouted out as the implication of this dawned on her. The road to the dam!

Her spirits lifted and resolution glinted in her dark eyes but she had no idea how far it was, how dangerous those tracks. She knew from Kip that the area around the dam had been carved from thick jungle and a stroll through the jungle was not a very happy thought. She would probably have to be rescued herself.

She jumped up at the sound of an engine as a lorry pulled out from behind the airport buildings and came rumbling slowly towards her, and she stood with determination as she saw the bright yellow body, the name in brilliant blue blazoned across the side. Mallory-Carter! Andrea stepped forward and stood firmly in the road. If this lorry was going to the dam then so was she, and nobody was going to stop her!

It was an African driving and he was clearly astonished at the way she stood in the middle of the road. He was only going slowly and at one point seemed to have decided to manoeuvre around her. She foiled him by side-stepping into his path and staring at his alarmed face. He stopped, but only, she thought, because he was undecided upon any other course of action.

'Are you going to the Kabala Dam?'

Andrea skipped round to the driver's door and hung on, quite decided that she was not going to be bypassed. He looked at her and said nothing, his eyes round, alarmed and embarrassed.

'Well, are you or aren't you?' she snapped, wanting to shake him to his senses.

'Yes. But——'

'No buts!' Andrea bit out firmly. 'Take me there too. The boss is expecting me,' she added with a burst of inspiration.

'OK, miss.' He moved to get out and help her, this small white woman who knew the boss, but Andrea wanted them out of there fast before any of the soldiers came to investigate.

'Stay put!' She whizzed round the lorry and hauled herself up, merely adding to his astonishment, his stare growing wider than ever. 'Go, go, go!' she advised and he nodded numbly but he obeyed. They were on their way and Andrea sat back, congratulating herself whole-heartedly. As a survivor in the face of hostility she wasn't doing too badly. From now on, *she* was going to be the one to be hostile, because she was on her way. The 'boss' was about to be put severely in his place.

The wind blew in her face—so did the dust for that matter—but it wasn't so hot when they were moving and she was reasonably close to her goal. Somebody had a whole lot of explaining to do, and the discomfort she was suffering would do nothing to soften her attitude. She wouldn't think about Kip because now she was near her aunt's thoughts seemed to be stealing her own mind away. If he were crippled—dead... She grimly sat up and tightened her lips. She wasn't the sort of person who lived in dread of the unknown. Kip would be there and she would rescue him and the boss would be told just where he got off!

It was unbelievable. Long before they arrived she could see the great towering walls of the dam rearing out of the jungle. Its height was frightening and she felt shaky when she thought of Kip working on this monster. Some great river would be let loose into here and then water would be readily available, but right now it was just an alien scar on the jungle-clad hills, the silence making it seem worse. She would have expected to hear noise, ma-chinery, engines, but there was nothing, no rumble of work in progress. The sounds of the jungle were all around her, and she stole a look at the impassive face of her driver and wondered if there was anyone at the dam at all. It was like waking up to find that most people had gone off-planet without telling you, and the feeling of unease she had had at the airport returned, stronger than ever.

There were people, though. The lorry pulled at last into an enormous clearing that had been gashed and scarred out of the jungle. It was hard-packed red mud, with the yellow digging equipment around it, all idle. There were trailers nearer to the edge of the trees and one large trailer that stood alone. Further away, Nissen huts stood apart; they might be where the men dined, or showered? Her thoughts did not dwell on any of this for long, though, because as she half jumped and half fell from the high lorry she was the focus of many eyes, all male, and then she was in the centre of a small but noisy crowd.

At any other time she would have been alarmed to be surrounded by so many men, but right now she was almost sagging with relief. They all seemed to be speaking at once and she couldn't help smiling even though she was worried. Her eyes scanned quickly for Kip, miraculously recovered, but he wasn't there and she couldn't get a word in at all.

They were English, Canadians, Australians, great tough men who were delighted with the sight of such beautiful fairness.

'Blimey! It's the opposite sex!'

'So you came for me at last!'

'I love you, whoever you are!'

It was all good-natured and boisterous and one man took pity on her confusion.

'Harry Carstairs—the foreman,' he said with a wide grin. 'You'd better have a good excuse for being here, miss. I hope you're not the Press because the boss——'

'Aw, Harry! Leave her alone. You're too old for her!'

It looked as if the friendly chatter would never stop and Andrea felt almost breathless. She also didn't miss the look in one or two pairs of eyes and her uneasiness began to come back as she fixed her gaze hopefully on Harry, the foreman. He was middle-aged, fatherly looking, and he was the one who suddenly squashed all the chatter, his words hissed out.

'Scat!' he muttered fiercely. 'Here's the boss!'

It was like a magic incantation. There was instant silence and Andrea raised her head from her intent and appealing gazing at Harry to see trouble heading her way with long, swinging strides.

This was a big man, her astonished eyes told her. He was towering over them before anyone had the chance to move and Andrea realised that she was not quite level with his shoulders. He was clad in khaki trousers that stretched across lean hips, his legs long and strong against the tough material. His shirt was the same, the sleeves rolled up to disclose powerful forearms that Andrea assumed dazedly could wrestle an ox.

She seemed to be staring at a powerful chest, too, and only by a great effort of will did she look upwards to encounter the eyes that glared down at her. They were tawny, a sort of burnished gold, utterly unusual, and she wondered light-headedly if a lion had eyes like that; she'd never taken the trouble to find out, and from the look in those tawny eyes it was all far too late now.

He had dark hair that looked as stormy as the rest of him, his skin was bronzed by the sun and he glared around, giving everyone the benefit of his furious displeasure, his hands on his lean hips, the hard muscles of his chest expanding as he strove to contain a ferocious rage.

'Are you all out of your minds?' he grated harshly, all that more menacing because he didn't shout. 'Get back to work! We've got *two days* and no longer!'

They went like so many subdued sheep, the looks in some of their eyes that had rather worried her utterly banished as other shades of thought intruded and Andrea was almost forgotten. The tawny eyes were turned solely on her then, the anger seemingly worse for one mind-stopping second before he turned to the foreman.

'Get the idiots back to work, Harry,' he bit out. 'Show them a woman and they lose all sense of self-preservation.' He glared down at Andrea again and one brown finger jabbed the air in her general direction. '*You!* Follow me!'

He turned on his heel and strode off, no doubt whatever in his mind apparently that she would obey. He was clearly used to unthinking obedience. Not only was he the boss, he was a hard, uncompromising man and she had no doubt whatever that he was responsible for Kip's trouble and her own discomfort. She seethed!

Following him consisted of trotting to even keep behind him and he made no sort of concession; he didn't even offer to carry her bag. Scurrying behind him with her shoulder-bag slipping down her arm and her grip full of clothes getting heavier by the second did nothing to endear him to Andrea. Her eyes burned vindictively at him as she watched the broad shoulders resentfully. Flies were buzzing round her, moisture slid into her eyes and off her chin and she had no free hand to wipe it away. She was not surprised that the flies kept clear of him. They had probably learned their lesson by now.

He was like a powerful machine gone berserk and she had never before been so conscious of her diminutive stature. Even so far in front of her he seemed to be towering over her. There was lithe strength in that angry, powerful frame and a raw, furious masculinity. He *bristled* with a sort of disgusting sexual authority that she had never seen before. He was MAN in block capitals.

He was sweating, the shoulders of his khaki shirt darkened by it, the material sticking to his back, and she curled her nose in distaste. The others had been sweating too—so was she for that matter—but she already hated this man for Kip's sake and she chalked it up against him.

He was making for the biggest trailer and that was another thing; clearly he kept the best for himself, a brute of a man. She put on a spurt and was almost directly behind him as he reached the door.

'In here!' He growled out the words and stepped aside, indicating the now open door of the trailer and Andrea cringed away from him, her face mirroring her aversion to his presence.

'So I'm not bandbox fresh, sweet as a lily!' he rasped. 'If you'd thought to inform me of your visit I would have donned the white tie!'

He met her gaze, glare for glare and she tightened her lips, stepping past him and climbing into the trailer.

She had to make a hasty reappraisal of her earlier thoughts when she was inside. It was an office as well as sleeping quarters and obviously the works manager would need an office. It didn't make her feel at all guilty, though, and she dropped her bag on the floor and looked round as somebody stopped close by to speak to him, delaying his entry.

The end near the door contained a rough desk and all the paraphernalia that paperwork required; the rest was extremely basic—a bunk bed, a huge fridge, a cooker and a table. There was a chair at the table and another at the desk and she assumed he had one knife, fork and spoon. He looked like that; one of everything and no trimmings. He was uncouth, a savage. Everything looked clean, though, and she would be able to sit with safety on one of the chairs—if he invited her to sit.

He stepped inside, slamming the door behind him, enclosing them in choking heat, and he looked bigger than ever, his eyes glittering like topaz in his hard, tanned face.

'What the hell do you think you're doing here?' he bit out furiously with no diversion for introductions and in spite of her determination to dress him down and get Kip out of here Andrea found her hands shaking. She gripped her shoulder-bag tightly and faced him head on.

'I've come to get Kip.'

'You've *what*?' His voice exploded into the stifling heat of the room, reverberating around her. 'God give me strength! A tiny little dolly-bird following him out here? I gave him credit for more taste.'

'Kip has more taste than you'll have if you live to be ninety, which I doubt, because you'll die of rage long before then! And I'm Kip's sister,' she added as he looked about to seize her and beat her up savagely. 'You can just tell me what you've done with him and I'll take him home!'

It gave him pause for thought, she could see that, but it did nothing to lessen his white-hot temper.

'So! You're the kid sister? What was the plan, to construct a litter and drag him back through the jungle? It's taking all your strength to hold that bag. How old are you—sixteen? Can't that aunt of yours keep you under control?'

He sounded so scathing and Andrea glared at him. *She* was the one with reason to be scathing. She resented the fact that he knew anything about her and even, for a moment, felt cross with Kip, who had obviously told him. This was the man who had sent half a telephone message and nothing more, she was quite sure of that. Everything about him said that he wouldn't be bothered to act in any kindly manner. His savagery was barely contained. At any moment he might throw her over his shoulder and stride back to the airport beating her all the way.

'What have you done with Kip?' she choked out furiously, dashing away the trickles of water than ran down her face. 'Which of these dirty huts have you used to contain him?'

'Very haughty,' he observed sarcastically, his dark brows meeting in a scowl. 'Your brother was flown out from Nairobi two days ago; by now your aunt will have had a cable and a letter and your brother will be tucked up in hospital in London at the company's expense. Because there's nobody, apparently, to curb your teenage enthusiasms when Kip is away, I now have *you* on my hands!'

'Oh!' Andrea just stared at him and the golden eyes narrowed to slits.

'A very inadequate answer, I would have thought. Lord knows what I'm going to do with a frisky girl until I can get you out of here!'

'I'm twenty-four,' she began, her rage somewhat dashed, 'and——'

'I'd have to see your birth certificate,' he sneered, interrupting rudely. 'All I know is that Kip has a kid sister, and you fit the bill down to the last silky curl. You should be locked up in whatever school you attend until your keeper collects you. I've got enough to do without taking care of slinky teenagers.'

Andrea rummaged in her bag and slapped her passport down in front of him, her face flushed and annoyed at his words.

'Twenty-four!' she snapped, snatching it back again. 'I may have acted hastily in coming out here but one unfinished telephone message is hardly adequate in face of my aunt's anxiety, not to mention my own. I would have expected better of a firm as big as Mallory-Carter. *And* I still don't know what happened to Kip; what sort of an accident, how bad he is. All you're capable of is raging and being rude.'

'His leg is broken in several places,' he informed her briefly, the eyes narrowed back to glittering anger, the dark eyebrows bunched together menacingly. 'He'll live and thrive and be back on the job in a few months.'

'Thank you for telling me—belatedly,' she said scornfully. 'If you could have brought yourself to let us know at once then I wouldn't have been out here in this disgusting place. Furthermore, I don't like your attitude and I'm quite sure the firm won't like it either. Neither Mr Mallory nor Mr Carter will approve of you when I report your behaviour.'

'Oh, I wouldn't bother doing that,' he suggested, his deep voice menacingly soft. 'I'll report myself and take anything that's coming to me for my insolence but I don't think it will be much.'

'You think wrongly,' Andrea informed him loftily, her small chin raised. 'Civilised people don't take kindly to this sort of thing.'

'Oh, I believe you, lady,' he assured her scathingly, his Canadian accent suddenly becoming apparent, 'but then, Carter is eighty and not given to bursts of reproach. *I'm* Mallory and, far from punishing myself, I've a mind to put you over my knee and belt seven bells out of you!'

CHAPTER TWO

'YOU—you can't be Mallory! Mr Mallory is a wealthy businessman; he wouldn't be out here in this—this——'

'Hell-hole?' he enquired, helpfully sardonic. 'I'm Kane Mallory all right and I'm out here because the project needs me.'

The name convinced her. Kip had written enthusiastically about his friend Kane but he had never mentioned that Kane was Mallory. No wonder everyone called him the boss and jumped rapidly when he was there. She was embarrassed into silence, but not for long.

'You could have phoned properly. If you had trouble you could have phoned again—at once!'

'On a non-existent line?' he enquired coldly. 'That call to your aunt was the last call out and I wish to hell it had been cut off before then. As it is, Kip is in England and I've got *you*!'

He made her feel about sixteen after all, a teenage nuisance. Nobody had ever reduced her to her size before in her life and she resented him bitterly, her brief embarrassment forgotten.

'Just give me transport to the airfield and I'll go now,' she snapped, her dark eyes filled with her resentment. 'I have no desire to be here. I'll get the next plane out.'

Apparently there was something in that statement that fuelled his temper further because he glared at her furiously.

'You're not going anywhere. In fact you're not moving from my side. Having you on my conscience is more

22

than a man could bear. I'd see that fragile little body
and that silky hair for the rest of my life.'

'Wh-what do you mean?' She stared up at him, her
face suddenly white and he grimaced sourly.

'Don't panic. I'm not keeping you for myself—
"finders keepers". There's a revolution in Madembi and
we're pulling out the day after tomorrow. It's the last
and the only plane out of here. You've come to rescue
Kip so gallantly. I hope your nerve holds out, because
he's the only one who's safe.'

The soldiers at the airport suddenly came into her
mind, the deserted street, the feeling that everyone had
fled.

'Then why was I allowed to land? Why did they let
me come here? The soldiers at the airport——'

'Lady, they're government troops. The airport is still
in government hands and we'd better pray that it remains so until our plane comes for us. If they scared
you, wait until you see the opposition! As to letting you
come here, they're expecting a miracle to save them. A
whole heap of foreign aid comes here and too many
sticky fingers are in it for them to let the world know
what's happening until it's actually happened. There are
one or two neighbouring states that feel pretty much the
same, maybe strongly enough to intervene. Right now,
though, you've waltzed into a revolution against a
democratically elected government and by the day after
tomorrow Okasi's murderous guerrillas will be here, or
very close.'

'How do you know they won't be here sooner?' She
stared at him in near horror and he looked utterly
scathing.

'Oh, my spies are everywhere,' he mocked. He looked
supremely powerful, sure of himself, a revolution nothing
to disturb him unduly. He might be a wealthy businessman but right at this moment, here in this stifling trailer,

all she could see was an arrogantly virile man, as dangerous as the jungle around them.

'W-what shall I do?'

Her appealing eyes and her shocked face seemed to take some of the heat out of his temper because his eyes slid over her thoughtfully.

'You'll leave with us when the plane comes and until then you'll become invisible. The men have too much to do without any thoughts of tawdry love-affairs.'

'They were only being friendly,' Andrea muttered, colour flooding back into her face under his long, assessing stare. 'I—I was glad of a few friendly faces.'

'Oh, I can imagine how friendly they felt. As a crowd, they're safe, especially with Harry there,' he commented coldly. 'Taken individually, though, I don't think that sassy tongue would help much. You stay with me. I'm not about to throw Kip's sister to the wolves and I can do without the aggro.'

Her dark eyes dropped away from his and she found she was incapable of looking back at him. She knew now what a pest she was. Even if he hadn't told her so thoroughly nastily she would have realised that getting her out of here was an extra responsibility he could well have managed without.

'I'm sorry,' she muttered, her eyes still looking intently at the floor. He made her feel small, helplessly female, and at the moment she was too stunned to resent it.

'Hmm! That remains to be seen. Let's hope you don't have to be too sorry.' He came over and stood looking down at her, tilting her chin impatiently when she refused to look up. 'You look all worn out and damp,' he commented wryly. 'I've got too much to do to see to you. I assume the hefty bag contains clothes. Stay in here and get a wash—use the sink. I'll try to get you a shower later. I haven't time to guard you now.'

'I can see to myself. I don't need guarding.'

'What do you suggest I do, tie up all the men? You get a wash here!' he finished almost violently.

'I'll be just as sticky two minutes after I've washed,' she reminded him, blinking her eyes as she was forced to meet his hard, golden stare.

The strong hand left her chin and he looked round, striding to a cupboard and taking out a fan.

'This should help,' he commented, switching it on, and Andrea felt at once the blissful cool waves that flowed from it.

'Why didn't you have it on?' she enquired shakily, her strength undermined by the feel of his hard fingers which still seemed to be at her delicate jawline. He had a way of reducing all the fire in her to nothing. The only fire was in her cheeks now and she had the irritated feeling that he knew.

'Too busy to bother,' he informed her cryptically. 'In any case, I'm used to the heat.' He glanced at her flushed cheeks and then strode to the door. 'You can lock the door and drop the blinds. I'll be about two hours; after that it will be too dark to bother about anything else today. There's plenty of cold drink in the fridge, food too if you're hungry.'

Andrea didn't seem to be capable of doing more than stare at him and his dark brows rose fractionally as he opened the door.

'Stop worrying, kid,' he murmured. 'I'll see to you.'

'Maybe that's what I'm worrying about,' she found her ready tongue saying, her face flooding with colour all over again as she realised it.

'Wrong combination,' he decided after a brief, assessing look at her that started at her legs and worked its way up comprehensively. 'I'm too big and you're too small. In any case, I like women with more substance

and I'm not altogether convinced that you're more than
a nubile teenager.'

His lips twisted wryly and he walked out, slamming
the door again, leaving her to her hot blushes. She heard
him stride away, everything about him forceful and aggressive. There was not much doubt who was the boss
here and she had travelled a very long way to put him
in his place. She gave a shaky little laugh. What a
mistake! If she annoyed him too much he would shake
her like a rat. She had the decided feeling that it was
only her relationship to Kip that had kept him from
physical violence already. The temper was like a
volcano—constantly bubbling.

She almost sprang on the door and locked it. He had
told her to do that and if now he had changed his mind
then it was too bad. The blinds took a little longer, because he had obviously not bothered with this re-
finement and they were mostly jammed, but she managed
it, peering out into the clearing through the slats before
letting the final one fall and leaving herself in the near
gloom.

Of the men she had seen when she arrived not one
was visible. Wherever he expected them to be, they were
surely there. Not, she mused, that they would dare do
otherwise. Kane Mallory was a very tough man and dis-
obedience would be far from the minds of any of them.
Apart from their jobs hanging on his approval, he looked
too forceful a character to be ignored.

He had made an impresson on her, she had to admit
that. With those tawny eyes intently on her she had quite
forgotten that he was unshaven, sweating and tough. She
had never met such a dynamic man, had not even
thought of anyone to compare with him. The men she
knew were almost all at the university, with a certain
suave air to them, a civilised veneer at least, and mostly
the civilisation ran very deep. Kane Mallory was all

potent male, a devastating animal magnetism about him that had finally got through to her even when she was raging at him. She didn't like him, and somewhere deep down she still struggled to put every ounce of blame on him, but he could not be ignored.

Andrea peered into the modern fridge and found it stocked with just about anything she could have wanted in the way of drinks or snacks. She was too tired and shaken to eat and she decided to save the drink for later, after she had washed. He had said two hours but she didn't fancy facing his temper if he came back and had to wait outside for her to finish getting ready; he would probably lift one of those powerful hands and smash the door in!

Diving into her bag for soap and clean underwear, she stripped off completely and gave herself a good wash-down at the sink, glorying in the feel of cold water. She didn't have a towel but she had no hesitation about searching for one of his and using it. She put on some thin cotton trousers and a matching blue top and then slid her feet into flat sandals before raising the blinds and turning to the fridge and her drink.

She felt almost human again, and she sat with a glass full of cold orange juice and pried into the papers on his desk with no hesitation whatever. She didn't under-stand one of them. They were far too technical, the drawings things she had seen often enough on Kip's desk at home, but somehow on a grander scale. There was a finished drawing of the Kabala Dam as it would look a long time from now and she was fascinated by the sheer beauty of the fine ink lines, the delicately added details. She wondered if Kane Mallory had done it himself.

His reading material was also a surprise. She had expected brightly coloured paperbacks, shockers, but she found only the classics and it just didn't fit in with his character. She was reading one when he came back and impatiently rattled the door which she had forgotten to unlock.

He didn't rave at her. Instead he stepped inside and muttered, 'Good girl. None of the men had any spare time but it was as well to keep the door locked.'

She hadn't. All she had done was forget to unlock it but she took the compliment—if that was what it was—and gave him a small tight smile as he straightened to his full height, having negotiated the doorway.

'I don't imagine they're *all* animals,' she said tartly, managing to convey that he was. 'It's useless trying to frighten me.'

'I'm glad you realise that I'm only trying,' he growled. 'I'm not trying very hard either. Maybe I'll put my mind to it.'

'Brute force is the lowest thing,' Andrea commented haughtily. Her tone ignited flames in the golden eyes.

'You have experience of it, Miss Forsythe? Care to show me your bruises?'

'You're a low-down, disgusting——!'

She gave a squeal of fear as his hands shot out and spanned her waist, tightening until she was breathless. Her eyes were wide with fright as the narrowed gaze held hers and he slowly lifted her into the air, looking up at her, his lips twisted with cold amusement, awareness of his potent masculinity in his taunting gaze.

She was like a doll in his hands, his strength counting her puny. His hands tightened and he lifted her higher, his strange golden eyes alive with devilry.

'Apologise,' he ordered softly, but she looked down at him, tightening her lips and shaking her head stubbornly, screaming as he tossed her up and caught her easily.

'Apologise.' His voice was silky soft but infinitely dangerous and she was well aware that she was at the mercy of a hard-eyed giant who had no scruples at all.

'I'm sorry.' She gasped it out and he lowered her slowly, letting her slide down his body until her feet touched the floor, the action so slow and lingering that she had no doubt at all what was on his mind. A shudder ran through her as he released her.

'Remorse is good for the soul. Feeling better now?' he enquired, his eyes skimming over her coolly, not missing the turmoil inside her. The fan had dried out her damp hair and she had brushed it back to its normal shining silkiness. It fell in gleaming waves to just below her shoulders and the tawny eyes lingered on it for a second.

'If you want to play games, then fine. Just remember, though, that I make my own rules.'

She refused to answer. How she was going to put up with him until the plane came was beyond her. He was dangerous, inhuman. She stared at him, dying to say something but uneasy about any reaction.

'Put it right out of your mind.'

For a second he looked into her dark eyes, seeing her resentment and ignoring it, threat at the back of his gaze, and then he turned away impatiently.

'I'll get a shower before we eat. Later I'll escort you over there and stand guard while you shower. The men come first, though; they're far more in need than you.'

'I can manage if water is scarce,' Andrea snapped, wondering where 'over there' was. 'I've already had a top-to-toe wash.'

'Interesting thought,' he mused sardonically, slanting her a gleaming look. His glance moved around the cleaned-up sink area. 'Not one drop of water splashed either—neat little thing.'

He ignored her bottled-in rage and picked up the towel she had used. It was almost dry by now and he unexpectedly held it to his face, breathing in the lingering perfume of her soap. His eyes were half closed as he looked at her.

'I see you borrowed my towel?'

'I—I'm sorry. I didn't have one and I saw you had others.' A wave of sheer fright hit her. There was a sensuous droop to his hard mouth, his nostrils flaring slightly, the towel still against his face. Was he as bad as his men? Was that why he was scrupulously keeping her here? The way he held the towel made her feel that he was almost breathing in the scent of her. Her skin shivered unexpectedly and she looked hastily away. 'I—I'm sorry,' she said again, filled with a great desire to placate him.

'That's all right. Don't apologise until I tell you. This will do. Maybe your delicate nature will rub off on me.'

The hard mouth twisted sardonically, sensuality quite gone, and he picked up some clothes, striding to the door and walking off. She actually ran to the window to watch him. The towel was over his shoulder and he stopped as someone called him, his lean height resting easily on strong legs, a peculiar grace about him that she hadn't noticed before. He laughed, the dark brows raised in amusement, and she stared at him, bewildered by her own feelings, gasping aloud when he half turned and looked back at the trailer.

Andrea moved hastily out of sight. There was a funny feeling inside her that certainly wasn't rage. She didn't like the idea of him using that towel after she had used it. It was somehow—intimate. The way he had held her towel to his face, breathed in the perfume, frightened her still. His half-closed eyes had frightened her too.

Idiot, she muttered to herself. Let him use a second-hand towel if he wanted to. It would have been worse if she had had to use it after him. He was just a rough man, animal, as bad as the other men. Nevertheless, it made her mind hang around the subject, imagining him

in the shower, that tough, powerful body being scrubbed
and then dried on her towel. She could imagine the
muscles on his back, the flat tough stomach, his lean
hips, strong legs. When he had slid her against him she
had felt his muscles contract. She went hot-faced and
fluttery, pulling herself up sharply. It was almost in-
decent! What was she doing dwelling on a man like that?
He was nothing more than a brute—Tarzan!

She suddenly felt oddly empty inside and hastily put
it down to hunger. She rummaged in the fridge, coming
up with the makings of a ham sandwich, walking round
aimlessly with it in her hand, keeping her mind firmly
under control and she was just finishing eating it when
he came back, catching her off guard, still brooding
about the situation.

'Tsk!' he reprimanded mockingly. 'Little girls
shouldn't eat between meals. You'll not want your dinner
and then you'll go to bed hungry and want to raid the
fridge in the night.'

He was infuriating! Andrea forgot her fright and her
unusual feelings and spun round to tell him off. She
stopped, stunned at the change in him. He had shaved
and showered and his hair was still damp but now
smoothly brushed, the dust gone, showing how gleamingly dark it was. His face was harshly handsome, the
tan now looking smooth and attractive, the impossible
tawny eyes more amber still.

Black jeans clung across his hips and a soft pale grey
cotton shirt moulded itself to his chest. Her mouth went
dry and she just went on staring at him as he watched
her with wry amusement.

She had never felt like just staring at a man before.
There was an element of leashed-in power about him,
reminiscent of the jungle outside, but he was twice as
dangerous as any primeval forest. Danger shone from
those golden eyes but she couldn't look away. There

really must be something wrong with her. The cave man
type was strictly out of her understanding, repulsive!
Silence hung between them like a dark curtain and he
prolonged it deliberately.

'You want me to introduce myself again?' Apparently
he was highly amused.

'Manners maketh man, not clothes,' she pointed out
tartly, a sharp phrase to cover her almost frantic feeling
of sexual recognition.

'In that case there's no hope for me,' he countered
ironically, walking slowly across to her. 'A crumb on
your lip,' he murmured, wiping it away with one fingertip. For such a big man his touch was incredibly light,
unnoticeable except that it seemed to shoot an electric
spark through Andrea, taking her breath away as his
fingertip lingered against her mouth, slightly probing
against the softness of her lower lip. She sprang from
him like a startled rabbit.

'Do you want me to get a meal ready? I—I mean
there's things in the fridge and—and . . .'

'No.' For a second he regarded her with an amused
quirk to his lips and then turned away, stacking his toilet
things on to the shelves. 'We all eat the evening meal
together. After a day on the dam the men can hardly be
expected to cook up a meal. We have a cook. He can
usually manage something reasonable. I just have one
or two things to do and then we'll go over to the hut
where we eat.'

He simply sat down at his desk and ignored her and
Andrea was at a loss what to do now. She found herself
watching him again, the way his dark head bent over
the desk. His hair was slightly curling in the back of the
neck. She pulled her gaze away a little desperately as it
began to wander stealthily to his broad shoulders. She
was thinking about the muscles beneath the shirt, about

the strength of his hands. Did she have malaria, some sickness?

She stared out of the window and then wandered around the room looking at almost anything rather than him. He made the room seem small, confining her, his presence everywhere. She began to inspect the walls for the first time, resolutely keeping her head turned away. There were maps and plans and she suddenly stopped dead.

'Oh, it's Kip!' Her startled exclamation as she found a photograph pinned to the wall just beside his desk drew his attention.

'Yes. The crew working on the dam. The three at the top are the main engineers. None of them here now. The other two flew out with Kip but I needed the rest of the men.' He looked up at her smiling face as she stared at the happy, bronzed face of her brother, Kip's fair hair, not as fair as her own, his dark eyes smiling back at her.

'You're pretty close to him, aren't you?'

'Yes. We've always been close. Losing our parents early in life drew us even closer together, I expect.' She was talking without thinking, forgetting who it was beside her for a second. 'Aunt Maureen brought us up but really I suppose we managed between us, the three of us; she's a bit—delicate.'

'Like you.'

'I'm not delicate!' She remembered who he was then, remembered how he had tossed her up in the air like a child, and she spun round in annoyance only to find him looking up at her seriously, his eyes on her delicately boned face.

'You look it, all that fragile bone-structure, that tiny frame. Andrea, isn't it?'

'How do you know?' She frowned down at him, inexplicably uneasy at his serious look. He smiled wryly.

'How could I not know? Kip's adored kid sister. At one time I thought I was going to be dragged home to meet you. Luckily I had to go back home to Canada.'

'Very fortunate,' Andrea said tightly, her imagination running riot, picturing him in her aunt's neat cottage, those long legs stretched out as he sat in one of the chintz-covered chairs. He would make the place seem smaller than ever.

'I thought so. I like Kip. It saved me the trouble of disappointing him.'

'Didn't anyone ever try to teach you any manners?' Andrea snapped and he swung lazily to his feet, towering over her, his eyes shuttered.

'Not that I remember. Perhaps later I'll let you try. Come on, I'll take you to dinner.'

'How very civilised! Do I need my evening bag?'

'Just a handkerchief to cry into if you get too uppity,' he warned darkly, taking her arm and propelling her to the door.

The dark had dropped with astonishing speed, no twilight at all, and arc lamps had come on around the compound, casting their shadows along the ground, hers small and slight, his gigantic, alarming, so that Andrea was very relieved to enter the bright lights of one of the Nissen huts and see the men standing around waiting for their meal. She didn't like him touching her and now his hand fell away as if he knew.

'They've all changed for dinner,' she murmured in astonishment, glad to have something to say. There was an air about him that made her feel he could read her every thought, as if this stranger knew her body language.

'Habit,' he assured her. 'It's easy enough in Africa to get into sloppy ways. The emphasis your fellow countrymen placed on changing for dinner in foreign parts wasn't so silly when looked at closely. Of course,' he added drily, 'I expect you've added some spice to the changing this time, everyone nicely scrubbed.'

She kept quiet, bearing in mind her thoughts as he had gone to get scrubbed, but apparently he put her rather flushed face down to the pleasure he was sure she was getting at being the focus of all eyes.

'Enjoy yourself,' he murmured quietly, 'but watch your step. They're tough men. We don't want any midnight prowlers calling on our silky little kitten.'

'You're a really uncouth man!' she snapped in a low voice, and he nodded unconcernedly.

'Very astute. You've really lived to be able to categorise me!'

He looked savagely annoyed again, but he didn't leave her side and she wasn't bothered now. She felt quite safe in the presence of large numbers and Harry Carstairs was a very fatherly figure. There were the same looks from some of the men although the looks were very muted in face of Kane Mallory's power and height. One in particular was watching her intently. Harry greeted her cheerfully, noting that she looked cooler, and she turned to him thankfully. She had been a little shocked to find that she had moved surreptitiously closer to Kane as the man had stared at her, and Harry was a very welcome port in this particular storm. She didn't want to move close to Kane Mallory. Sometimes he seemed to be almost surrounding her.

Kane introduced her laconically, his voice sufficiently raised to carry to everyone.

'Andrea Forsythe, Kip's sister,' he announced with just a touch of menace, and it had the desired effect.

'Aw! 'Struth! You missed him!' Harry's voice was all commiseration and she expected some sarcastic comment from Kane Mallory but he surprised her.

'Unfortunate but true. She'll leave with us, though, and no harm done.'

'Let's hope so,' Harry commented worriedly.

Getting out of Madembi safely was the main subject of conversation among the men until Kane noticed Andrea's face and cut the speculation short impatiently. Thereafter the meal proceeded pleasantly, everyone on their best behaviour. They knew who she was and could see that she was firmly under the protection of the boss. Andrea wasn't quite sure of the protection bit. The others looked as if a tongue-lashing would subdue them and she was very good at that. Kane Mallory was not a man who could be subdued at all. The way he moved, the way he looked, those golden eyes: everything about him spoke of raw power, untameable.

The man who had been watching her moved closer as they prepared to leave—apparently he was not quite subdued enough—but Kane snapped a cold look at him and took Andrea's arm, almost marching her out, Harry walking with them.

'Do you reckon we'll finish in time?' Harry asked quietly.

'We don't have a lot of choice,' Kane muttered. 'We've got tomorrow. I want everything done before that plane comes in and when it does you'll all leave before me,' he added quietly. 'I'll stay to do what's necessary and catch you up.'

'OK, but I think . . .'

'We've been over this, Harry!' Kane said curtly, and turned Andrea away. '*She'll* be with you. I don't want any arguments.'

By that Andrea assumed that he meant her and she walked silently for a while as they returned to the big trailer.

'Aren't you leaving on the same plane?' she asked quietly.

'I am.' His curt voice told her to keep quiet but it wasn't really her nature.

'Then why...?'

'I've got things to do here at the last minute.'

'But——'

'Leave it,' he rasped. 'It's not "little girl" business and I'm merely tolerating you at the moment. Your unexpected arrival has not filled me with glee and I'm certain that after a while you will no longer amuse me, so keep out of my affairs.'

'With pleasure!' Andrea snapped, hatred seething back into her bloodstream. Whatever he was wearing, shaven or not, sweating or not, this was a rough, rude man. His sensuality was probably because he had just been released from a zoo!

His attitude when they were back in his trailer didn't help either.

'Where shall I sleep?' Andrea asked coldly, wanting to get wherever she was going and see the back of him.

'Right here.'

She looked at him in surprise; such chivalry didn't seem to fit.

'I assume that Kip had a trailer. I'll sleep there,' she said firmly, her small chin raised, showing him she wanted no favours.

'And curl up with two other fellows?' he rasped, a nasty and altogether uncalled-for contempt in his face. 'Kip shared a trailer as they all do. You'll sleep here!'

'Wh—what about you? I—I don't want to push you out—take your place...'

'I sleep here too.'

Andrea blinked in astonishment for a second, her earlier thoughts flooding back into her mind. So he *was* as bad as the men! They had backed off because...! She exploded into righteous wrath, her dark eyes pools of scorn and fury.

'So it's all right for me to curl up with *you* then but not with the others? Let me tell you that——'

'You want to curl up with me?' he interrupted with irritating, mocking surprise, one dark brow tilted. 'I'm immune, child—and they know it. They don't expect romance from me.'

'I have no desire to curl up with you and I'm not a child!' Andrea stormed, red-faced. 'I have a degree already and I'm studying for my doctorate at Oxford.'

His lips tilted in amusement and he gave her a wry glance that made her feel like Boastful Bertie.

'Very well, madam.'

'I preferred it when you called me lady in that vulgar way you have!' Andrea snapped, her embarrassment choking her and the amber eyes narrowed alarmingly.

'Watch your step with me, pint-size,' he growled. 'I'll call you anything I damned well choose. Just get it into that silky head that your safety lies in my hands, now and from now on until I get you out of here and back into the fluttering hands of Auntie! Next time, maybe, I'll toss you straight through the roof—or not let you go,' he added softly.

Andrea turned away furiously, unable to look back into those stunning eyes. She supposed he was right but he made her so wild with rage that she wanted to beat him senseless; not that anyone could—he would grasp them with one hand and shake the life out of them. And wasn't he threatening her with brute force?

'I've got to see Harry,' he announced coldly when she refused to turn back to face him. 'You stay here and get control of that childish temper. When I come back we'll see where you're going to sleep.'

He walked out, slamming the door as usual, and Andrea got her feelings under control. Really she had never hated anyone so much in her whole life. In fact she had never hated anyone in her whole life. Kane

Mallory was a first in everything. She pushed out of her mind the fact that he was also the first man she had stared at almost hungrily. It wasn't something to dwell on.

CHAPTER THREE

ANDREA was stifled but she didn't put the fan on; instead she defied Kane by stepping outside the moment he had gone. She walked to a pool of shadow and stood there breathing in the night air, listening to the night sounds of the surrounding forest. There was something sinisterly beautiful about it. She could understand why he reminded her of it.

She had never met a man she could not wind round her little finger. Her diminutive size had deceived so many and in many ways she was contemptuous of them, only recognising their brain power. Kane Mallory was outside her experience, beyond her comprehension, because under that sleek animal power there lurked a brain to match and better her own, she felt uneasily sure of that.

She made a great effort and thrust him out of her mind, leaning against the side of the trailer and wondering how Kip was. He was safe at any rate and although his leg was badly broken he would fully recover. Aunt Maureen would know by now and she would be worried frantic about *her*. So would Kip. He was still her big brother, and acted like that if need be. She bit her lip. Kip would be annoyed at her impulsive decision to come here. His annoyance would surface when she was safe. He could get quite annoyed sometimes, though never as annoyed as Kane Mallory. She had never met anyone with such a violent temper.

'What the hell are you doing out here? I thought I told you to stay inside?' He appeared so suddenly, so silently that Andrea gave a faint cry of alarm and flinched away.

'What's the matter? What's frightened you?' He grabbed both her arms and glared at her suspiciously.

'*You* have!' She snatched her arms away—at least she tried to. 'You appeared out of the night like the devil and started shouting at me and——'

'Be thankful it was me that appeared, not some other devil,' he rasped. 'I've warned you more than once.'

'I hid myself in the shadows.'

'And I saw you clear across the compound. You can't conceal hair like that. It's a liability when you're hiding.' He looked a little less annoyed and suddenly reached out to lift her hair away from her shoulders, letting the silken length of it stream through his fingers, his eyes curiously intent as if it fascinated him. He dropped it as suddenly, glaring down at her as if she had asked him to fondle her hair. 'Come inside!' he snapped, and she knew better than to disobey. His fingers had brushed her neck and her heart was beating wildly. If he was an animal he had plenty of magnetism.

'Oh!' A flash of light, infinitesimal and brilliant, caught her eyes and she stopped suddenly. It came again, and then more, and Andrea watched open-mouthed.

'Now what?' He turned back impatiently and then his eyes followed hers and he laughed softly, a husky, dark sound that shivered along her nerve-ends.

'Fireflies,' he enlightened her, stopping to watch with her, letting her stare her fill at the dancing specks of light that seemed to fill the darkened area close to the trees.

'How beautiful. Don't you think they're beautiful?' she appealed to him, forgetting their antagonism and looking up into his cynical face.

'Maybe.' He looked down at her entranced expression, her parted lips, and then watched with her for a few seconds more.

'They're ethereal, just light, like spirits,' she breathed solemnly, her face spellbound. 'It's magical.'

He gave a grunt of exasperation and strode forward, his hand suddenly flashing out as swiftly as the dancing lights, enclosing one and holding it for her to see. It was a small dark bug, nothing ethereal about it at all.

'A soft-bodied, nocturnal beetle of the family Lampyridae, with light-producing abdominal organs,' he announced with cynical exactitude.

'You're hateful!' Andrea turned away quickly as he let it go, all the enchantment wiped from her face. She was shocked at her own feeling of dismay that he had not felt what she had felt, that he had dismissed the magic. 'You spoil everything. I bet you pulled wings off butterflies when you were small!'

'I thought you were a dedicated student, studying for a doctorate? What's it in, fairy-tales? I expected you to have a trained scientific mind.'

'If it has to be like yours, then——'

Andrea stopped again as she saw, over his shoulder, the rising of the full moon. It seemed to lift like a giant over the tall trees, bigger than she had ever seen it, unreal, blood-red and quite frightening.

'Now that really *is* something,' he commented, turning to follow her awe-stricken gaze.

'It—it's alarming, not true. Look at the colour. I never thought the moon would scare me!'

She forgot to be annoyed and he came to stand beside her, no longer mocking.

'Nothing to be scared about. It's just the moon. The colour is caused because of a sandstorm.'

'Near here?'

'No, of course not. Probably the Sahara, a long, long way off.' He looked down at her and took her arm, turning her away. 'Come inside before you frighten yourself to death. You're going to be more of a responsibility than I imagined. The sassy tongue obviously covers a geat deal of fear.'

'I'm not scared of anything...!' Andrea began, stopping in the lighted doorway to glare up at him, determined to let not one insult pass unchallenged now.

Two strong hands spanned her tiny waist, convincing her that he was right about fear.

'In!' he commanded, tossing her casually into the trailer. 'The show is over. Let's get you to sleep and out of my hair.'

'You,' Andrea raged, 'would make the most abominable husband imaginable!'

She had no idea why she had chosen that particular insult and for a second a look flashed across his face that scared her and she thought she had gone too far this time. He shrugged and turned away.

'I told you, child, I'm immune.'

She didn't say anything about being called a child. That fleeting look had held something she didn't understand and she wasn't about to invite more trouble than she could handle. Maybe some woman had hurt him and that was why he was so awful? It was hard to imagine the sort of woman who could hurt Kane Mallory, though; she would have to be an Amazon. He looked as if he would have the monopoly on hurting.

'Shall I sleep in that bunk?' she enquired worriedly when he said nothing at all more, her irrepressible character somewhat subdued.

'Well, normally it would be expected,' he drawled sardonically, 'but then it's the only one and I'm not quite normal as you keep pointing out. I'm also six feet two and have no fancy for sleeping on a camp-bed. Therefore, you have the camp-bed and I have the bunk.'

'A—a camp-bed is close to the ground,' Andrea assured him anxiously, her remark drawing his mocking gaze back to her.

'Which is as well. You're too brittle-boned to survive a fall from more than a few inches.'

'I'm not about to fall out of bed,' she said hurriedly. 'I was thinking of bugs and—and things.'

'Ah! The terror again? My, my, Miss Forsythe, you *do* surprise me. A lady of your spirit so filled with fears. There are no bugs or related objects in my trailer. Sleep in the certain knowledge of that.'

He hauled out a camp-bed and proceeded to make it up for her and she stood watching with mounting alarm.

'But how can I get undressed?'

'I'll turn my back and count to any number you care to mention.' He sighed. 'Do you think we could settle now? I've got a hell of a lot to do tomorrow and at this rate we'll still be here arguing the toss when day breaks.' He turned his back and she suddenly thought he looked tired, surprised that it made her feel guilty. She wasn't doing too well as an avenging angel.

'I'll tell you when to turn,' Andrea said hurriedly, and then she stripped off to her panties and dived into the camp-bed with great speed.

He made no comment when she told him rather timidly that she was ready, and her heart took off alarmingly when he began to unfasten the grey sports shirt. He just stood there unfastening buttons slowly, looking down at her as if he was thinking unspeakable thoughts.

'No need for maidenly panic,' he assured her drily as she stared at him in horror, unable to look away, her eyes seemingly fastened to the broad, tanned chest that rippled with muscles, a shadow of dark hair across it. 'For the finale I'll put off the lights.'

Her eyes locked with his, two dark pools of panic that amused him into a smile, his white teeth brilliant against his tanned face.

'You could close your eyes now—if you're capable.'

She blushed furiously, shutting her eyes tightly, hearing the lights go out and then hearing him continue to undress.

'Goodnight, Andrea.' His voice was softly mocking and she didn't answer; she didn't think her own voice was up to it. She had never before wanted to simply watch a man, to see the rippling muscles disclosed. Her face was hot against the coarse pillow.

Andrea slept deeply. The flight had been a long one and the events that had followed had all combined to exhaust her. Shaken nerves and sheer irritation had kept her going the previous evening but once in the silent trailer, tucked up in the camp-bed, her exhaustion caught up with her. At first she listened worriedly for any sign that Kane was about to leave his bunk, but he seemed to sleep the moment his head touched the hard pillow and the sound of his steady breathing made her feel inexplicably safe.

When she woke up it was bright daylight and she looked round a little anxiously, relieved to find that Kane was gone and not surprised at that when she discovered that it was almost nine o'clock. She got out of bed quickly and went to lock the door, but he had dropped the latch as he left and she slipped the bolt on. The blinds were still lowered from the previous night and she was able to wash with a feeling of security.

She was hungry and made herself a substantial breakfast, washed the dishes and then found herself at a loose end. Kane must have gone out without eating because there was no sign of his dishes and nothing for her to do except tidy away the camp-bed. She raised the blinds and found the sunny compound too much to resist.

Nobody was about and she knew that they would all be busy this last day so she slipped outside and began a careful exploration. The nearby jungle deterred her. It looked altogether too dangerous—not a walk in the woods—but she had the greatest satisfaction in peering into every open door, the showers, the canteen and the largest hut that was some sort of store.

When she heard the noise of an engine she was quite a way from Kane's trailer and the thought rather alarmed her, a feeling she did not welcome. She hated being dependent on anyone, especially on Kane Mallory. She deliberately sauntered back, telling herself that she would not be driven to running to hide. Kane was just the sort of man to scare her on purpose.

A yellow dump truck pulled into the compound and she felt less sure of her own ability to take care of herself when she saw that the driver was the man who had persistently stared at her the night before. She kept on walking but he was right across her path and he switched off the engine as she came closer, leaning back in his seat to watch her insolently. He wasn't as big as Kane but he was big nevertheless and she was pleased to see that he made no move to leave his truck. She was fast on her feet and quite prepared to make a run for it if necessary.

'Well, hello,' he greeted, his eyes roaming over her unpleasantly. 'I can see that I've got you to myself.'

'For about half a second until I walk past,' she said coolly. 'I'm just on my way back to the trailer.'

'Kane's trailer, yeah! I'm not surprised he kept you for himself. You're quite something.'

'What do you mean?' Andrea spun round and faced him angrily, thoughts of flight banished. 'I was in Kane's trailer for my own protection and seeing you I can understand his anxiety. I had the camp-bed.'

'The camp-bed,' he jeered. 'His anxiety was to have you himself, daintily beside him in that bunk, and I can understand why.'

'How dare you?' Andrea snapped. 'The other trailers have several men in them.'

'What about your brother's trailer? There were two other men with him, both engineers. They left with him; it's only us roughnecks that had to stay and do the dirty work. Don't come the high and mighty with me. There was an empty trailer and you stayed with Kane.' His eyes roamed over her insinuatingly. 'I bet he enjoyed you, a great powerful man like that and you so tiny. Did he satisfy you?'

Andrea was white with anger, shamed by his words, and she glared at him, her eyes almost black with rage.

'Ask Kane,' she choked out, 'because I'll tell him what you said the moment he gets back. And if you so much as look in my direction again, I'll get the nearest heavy object and knock your head clean off!'

She stormed back to the trailer and bolted the door, dropping the blinds and then sitting down abruptly, her whole body shaken with rage and humiliation. She could remember perfectly well that Kane had mentioned the other two engineers leaving with Kip. She had never re-alised that they all shared one trailer. He had lied to her, kept her here to humiliate her because she had come out unexpectedly and uninvited. No doubt he resented her way of answering back and this was his nasty masculine way of punishing her. She hated him so much that she shook with it!

He came back half an hour later and by that time she had worked herself up into white heat. When he rattled the handle she stormed across to open the door, stepping back and then staring at him with intense dislike, her eyes two enormous pools of hatred.

It surprised him.

'I can see your sleep didn't do you a bit of good,' he commented drily, his eyes on her furious face. 'How odd. You were sleeping like a little silver lamb when I left.'

'You liar! You unspeakable pig!' she shouted, and his eyes opened wide and then narrowed to glittering menace.

'You'd better follow that up with one of your apologies while you still can,' he threatened, 'because I've got more to do than play games with you this morning.'

'Maybe you'd better call the men together and announce that we didn't play any games last night,' she raged. 'I've just been insulted as I've never been insulted before in my life and you're to blame!'

'What are you talking about?' He stepped closer and she backed off rapidly.

'Don't you touch me, you hideous brute!'

'I'll shake the life out of you if you don't start explaining and stop all this nonsense!' he rasped, looking quite capable of doing it.

'You told me the other trailers had men in them. You lied. That creep who was watching me last night told me that Kip shared with two engineers, the two you told me had left. That leaves one trailer empty but I had to share this one with you. He thinks that... He asked me if——'

'What did he ask you?' He barked out the question and Andrea flushed, embarrassment riding over rage.

'I—I'm not about to tell you!'

'Then you're about to get that neat little backside paddled,' he informed her angrily. 'I'm quite aware that your head is full of humorous stories!'

'It wasn't humorous. He—he said you were big and he asked me if——'

'Stop right there. I can imagine what he asked you,' Kane grated, fury on his face. 'Don't bother to enlighten me. I'll deal with him!'

'You brought it on, lying about that trailer. Every one of the men will be thinking the same thing, looking at me as if I'm——'

He grabbed her arm and swung her to the door, striding out across the empty compound and dragging her along behind him. She was almost pulled off her feet, running to keep upright, breathless and enraged when he stopped at one trailer and threw open the door.

'Kip's trailer! An empty trailer, Miss Forsythe!' he bit out. 'Note its position, isolated and quiet.' He swung her to the door and wrenched it back. 'Note the door, no lock, no blinds to the windows. You fancied sleeping here? You wanted to be a target for men such as Sutherland?'

Andrea stood silently, her arm still enclosed in his powerful hand, his fingers bruising. Everything he said was true, and the very thought of sleeping here alone with men like that close by terrified her.

'You could have told me—explained——' she began, but she got no further.

'Explained? To *you*? You're the most wilful, headstrong female I've ever set eyes on. No, I didn't explain because as soon as I was asleep you would have sneaked off and got yourself settled in here, smugly sure that you were doing the right thing! You've been insulted in broad daylight when somebody else was likely to come into the camp at any time. What do you think would have happened in the middle of the night with you dead to the world and an unwelcome guest in here?'

'I—I'm sorry,' she muttered but he looked ready to explode with rage and he took her shoulders, wrenching her round to face his furious amber eyes.

'With a temper like yours you'd better learn that phrase off by heart while you're near me,' he grated. His hands tightened to cruelty. 'And call me the things you called me ever again and you'll eat the words letter by letter!'

He took her arm and marched back to the trailer and she didn't care at all that she had to run to keep up. Her own words were still in her mind and she hadn't the faintest idea how she was going to make up for the insults she had hurled at him.

He pushed her inside and then ignored her, searching his desk with increasing rage.

'I'm sorry,' she offered again tremulously. 'He said so many awful things to me and I——'

'And you decided to say awful things to me, just to even the score?' he bit out angrily, turning blazing eyes on her.

She burst into tears. She had had enough shocks for one day and her own temper had left her very shaken.

'I've said I'm sorry,' she wailed. 'What do you want me to do, crawl around the floor?'

She searched frantically for a handkerchief, jumping in alarm when he came up and wiped her tears himself. She was shivering with reaction, reaction from his violent temper and equally violent handling and reaction because she had lost control of her own temper.

'Stop crying.' He pulled her into his arms and stroked his hand down her hair. 'You're a big nuisance for such a small object.' He tilted her face and wiped away the remaining tears with his thumb. 'I bet you were a beautiful baby and yelled your head off when you couldn't have your own way.'

'If you'd heard that man——' she began defensively, and he let her go, his face darkening.

'I didn't need to hear him. I've got a good imagination. He'll hear *me*! What were you doing outside?' he suddenly asked, turning back to her with further menace.

'There was nobody there,' she got out quickly, excuses being scarce.

One cynical eyebrow lifted but he made no comment except, 'Going out again?'

'No.' She shuddered and sat down and he turned back to his desk, his face frustrated.

'I'm glad you came back,' she placated. 'I didn't think you would.'

'I forgot something,' he snapped.

'Oh. Can I help? What was it?'

'I've damned well forgotten!' He glared at her and made for the door. 'You can make some lunch for noon,' he added irascibly. 'I'm going to the village this afternoon. *You're* coming with me!'

She just nodded dutifully and he gave her an exasperated look before he slammed the door. She almost fell on it and bolted it. Nobody was about to get the chance to sneak up on her. She was going to stick to Kane like glue until that plane got her out of here.

Andrea glanced nervously at the clock as lunchtime approached. She had gone to a lot of trouble to placate Kane and she was hot in spite of the fan. She had used all her ingenuity with the things in the fridge and all her patience with the two gas rings. There was a risotto waiting for him and if he was late it would be ruined.

He came right on time and she rushed to open the door, giving him a shaky smile. It earned her a sardonic glance.

'All friends, I see,' he drawled. 'Jolly good companions.'

It removed her smile and the friendly overtures were over. 'Get your lunch or it will be ruined,' she muttered angrily.

'Now, now,' he mocked as he went to wash at the sink. 'No scolding, Miss Forsythe. I'm rushing to do your bidding.'

She served it up without further comment and he ate it in silence, looking up at her from beneath dark brows when he had finished.

'I know that took some getting ready in these conditions. It was the best thing I've eaten since I came out here but you needn't have gone to such lengths. A sandwich would have done.'

'You said lunch. I made lunch,' she muttered, her face downcast. It suddenly hurt to be constantly battling and anyway, she relied on him, she reminded herself, pushing the idea of being hurt out of her mind with anxious rapidity.

'Don't try to please me, Andrea,' he said quietly. 'Just keep up the skirmishes. That's exactly what I want.'

She hadn't the faintest idea what he was talking about and she glanced up in surprise to find his face tight and his eyes on her silky hair.

'Tie your hair back,' he said abruptly, standing and putting the dishes in the sink. 'We're going on a jungle path to the village and it's not a good idea to have your hair waving like a silver banner.'

He was unfathomable. She stood and looked at him but he ignored her and simply waited until she had found a piece of ribbon in her bag and tied her hair into a high ponytail.

'Splendid,' he commented, his lips twisted wryly. 'You're like a silver flower, that slender neck all vulnerable. Maybe I should wrap you up and put you in my pocket.'

He made her blush but she faced him.

'You don't need to take me with you,' she said with quiet dignity. 'I can lock myself in here again. I only have to manage until tomorrow.'

'Maybe I can't bear to let you out of my sight,' he said drily, sarcasm on his face. 'Maybe tomorrow will come much too soon.'

His caustic mockery annoyed her but she held her tongue. He was *not* going to get her angry. She needed his protection and she was all set to get it. If he thought she looked vulnerable he would be just that bit more careful.

Not far out of the camp they turned on to a track that led into the trees and Andrea was fascinated as they drove slowly through the dappled sunlight. The humid heat was forgotten for a while as she gazed about. The noise of the jungle was loud and unexpected. There was the constant sound of birdsong, excited chattering and strange calls from creatures she could not see, weird and sudden screams that filled the air from time to time and the majesty of the towering trees all around them.

A small band of monkeys moved inquisitively with them, leaping from one branch to the next, their bright eyes watching and Andrea was entranced.

'Monkeys! Aren't they delightful?'

'At the risk of dashing your enchantment yet again, I'd better remind you that they're delightful at a distance only,' Kane grunted, his eyes on the track. 'Earlier in the year one of my men had thirty stitches by being delighted with monkeys. He decided to keep a pet, fed it and finally caught it. A monkey has four hands to grip you and a lot of teeth to bite you. It ended up taming *him*!'

It made Andrea look at them warily and he glanced across at her with a twisted smile.

'Going to tell me that I spoil everything?'

'No. I take your point. You're the expert, after all. In any case, I'm not romantically minded.'

'Aren't you?' The golden eyes flared over her for a second. 'You're like something that's stepped from the pages of a book, a fairy-tale book. I wouldn't like you to have to survive out here. Lord knows how you survive anywhere. You need a man to tuck you under his arm.'

'I'm extremely independent,' Andrea informed him, her face flushed. 'Even Kip has never really had to care for me, although he's always tried to.'

'I said a man, not a brother. You need someone to hold your hand, tell you when it's bedtime and carry you there.'

'Oh, and how do you know there isn't someone already?' she asked, red-faced and trying to look worldly.

He grinned to himself, his eyes on the track.

'You live in books and high ideals. Life simply hasn't touched you. Let's hope that when it does it touches you kindly.'

It was a conversation she didn't want to pursue, and in any case Kane was silent after that, only speaking when he had to.

The village was bigger than she had expected. The street that went through it was merely a continuation of the track but there was a sort of walkway made from rough planks and the houses too were wooden, very little more than crude huts but not the primitive dwellings she had imagined.

At the sound of the Land Rover they were surrounded by children who obviously knew Kane, and as he got out and went to the main house they ran along beside him, chattering. Andrea was a little surprised to see them so easy in his company and she stayed in the vehicle, watching as he slowed to let them keep pace with him, his face amused as he talked to the oldest boy.

It was a little while before he came back and when he did it was to find Andrea surrounded by small interested faces because the children had come back to the Land Rover.

'I know what they mean now about being the centre of attention,' she said with a smile as Kane reversed and moved off.

'Apparently they were having similar thoughts to the ones I had last night,' he murmured. 'They wanted to know if your hair was real. They've seen plenty of white women—this village isn't far from the town—but you're the first one with hair like silver.'

'I'm beginning to feel like a freak,' Andrea laughed.

'You're unusual,' he conceded. His voice was low and thoughtful and she had a frantic desire to turn the conversation in other directions.

'Did you get what you came for?'

'Yes. I know more or less where Okasi's gang are. They're heading this way.'

'W-was that one of your spies?' Andrea asked, alarm flooding through her at the thought of the rebels moving relentlessly forward.

'It's a villager who gets about,' Kane said with a tight smile. 'His brother is the one who drives our lorry back and forth for supplies. We all know Okasi is coming here. What we need to know is when. After tomorrow morning,' he added grimly, 'he can come and be damned!'

He was pretty silent after that, and when they got back he went off again until dinner-time, and it was only as they entered the hut where the evening meal was served that Andrea had to steel herself to face her opponent of this morning, the nasty, insulting Sutherland.

He wasn't there and there was an unusual quiet about the men, their eyes turned in her direction rarely and then to smile at her with a great deal of restraint and respect. Harry was the only normal person there and she began to wonder what had happened.

A latecomer slid into his seat and began to catch up with the eating, glancing at the seat opposite.

'Where's Sutherland? He's missing the steak. Not like him.'

There was utter silence and Andrea risked a look at the others from beneath her lashes. They were not looking at her and a few lips were twitching with tightly-held-in amusement. Kane looked totally enigmatic, continuing to eat his meal as if nobody had spoken at all.

It was Harry who finally answered. 'Sutherland's dining in his trailer. He's got his steak. He's wearing it.'

There were several men who unexpectedly choked and the latecomer looked at them and then at Harry, his face puzzled.

'Bad eye,' Harry said solicitously. It seemed to dawn on the man then. He glanced round and met a few amused eyes. He glanced at Andrea and then at Kane, who ignored everything. Nobody mentioned it again.

On the way back to the trailer, Andrea was filled with remorse. Kane was walking quietly beside her and she felt he was deliberately ignoring her because he was angry.

'I've caused a lot of trouble,' she admitted in a low voice.

'Oh, not too much,' he assured her easily. 'Women cause trouble when there's a gang of isolated men. Surely you didn't expect to go unnoticed?'

'If I'd done everything you told me to do...I'm sorry.'

'Stop saying that. I told you to say it when I ordered it,' he drawled. 'Keep up the battle, Andrea. It's what I want. I told you that too.'

She felt extremely subdued and at the door of the trailer Kane stopped and looked down at her.

'Want to see the fireflies?' he asked mockingly, adding, when she shook her head, 'The moon?'

'No, thank you.'

He laughed and allowed her to precede him into the trailer.

'Then I think it's bedtime. You've got the whole place to yourself for fifteen minutes.' He paused at the door on his way out. 'No need to lock up. I can guarantee no prowlers.'

She was sure he could. He went and she did exactly as she had done the previous night; undressed to her panties and slid into the camp-bed. When he came back in she was peering at him over the blankets and he seemed to find it all very amusing.

'I ought to have a photograph of that, to remind me of you in the long years ahead,' he mocked.

'You certainly help me to feel like a freak,' Andrea muttered.

'I'm concerned with helping to keep you in one piece,' he growled. 'I just have this night to live through and you'll be back in Kip's safe keeping, or Auntie's.' He proceeded to unbutton his shirt, a replay of the previous night and she turned her head away quickly.

'Will we be safe, do you think?' she asked a little breathlessly, the same turmoil entering her veins as he stood and looked down at her.

'All being well. Scared?'

'I suppose so. A bit. I keep thinking of those rebels getting closer.'

'They're not here yet,' he assured her. 'Keep calm. Do you want me to tuck you in?' he added mockingly, and she was irritated beyond words. Why couldn't he hold a normal conversation, discuss it with her, set her mind at rest? Instead he was constantly either raging or taunting.

'Oh, yes, please,' she said in her best little-girl voice, a cutting mockery in her voice too.

'Very well.'

To her horror he crouched beside the bed and when she looked round in fright he was looking at her tauntingly, his shirt unbuttoned to the waist, the muscles of his chest rippling with power. He proceeded to tuck in the blankets, meeting her irritated stare with a great deal of false surprise.

'You asked me to,' he reminded her. 'Your wish is my command, my lady.'

She opened her mouth to give him a piece of her mind but he bent his head forward and let his lips glide slowly over hers before looking at her tauntingly.

'Just to remind you of what I said,' he told her. 'You need a man to tuck you up and kiss you goodnight. When you get back, find one. With a temper like yours and so much splendid brain power you could end up as an old maid.'

He flipped off the lights before she could reply and, in any case, her lips seemed to be on fire. That kiss had done something unexpected to her. She was shaking.

'Goodnight, Andrea.' There was laughter at the back of his voice, and this time she tightened her lips together and turned angrily on her side. He was impossible. The strange turmoil inside her must surely be revulsion? How could it be anything else?

Oddly enough, she slept like a log, an inexplicable feeling of safety stealing over her. Nobody would challenge Kane Mallory, and she believed him when he said that he was immune. Thinking rationally about things, she decided that he disliked her as much as she disliked him, despised her too in his different way. The thought of his strange topaz eyes was still in her mind as she slid into a dreamless sleep, but they didn't scare her at all.

CHAPTER FOUR

'ANDREA!'

When she opened her eyes Kane was bending over her; it was broad daylight and his golden gaze was the first thing she saw.

'What is it?' She looked at him puzzled for a moment, a little disorientated.

'What it is is morning,' he said brusquely, the mockery of the previous night gone. 'I'm going out for about ten minutes. You've got that time to get up, get ready and produce breakfast for two. The last flight out of here leaves in two hours and there's the drive to the airfield.'

'Oh! Right!' Andrea struggled upright quickly, only remembering that she didn't have the sophistication of a nightie when his eyes widened. She slid back under the blankets, but not before his eyes had fastened vibrantly on her tilted rose-tipped breasts. His lips were slightly parted and he took a deep breath as he looked at her red face, his teeth snapping together.

'If this is how the day begins, heaven knows how it's going to end!' he muttered between his teeth, his eyes lingering on the curve of breasts just concealed now. He stood up and looked down at her in annoyance. 'I'm going, so rise and shine and don't bother to tidy up in any little woman way. All this is being abandoned. Leave the camp-bed and everything else. Get breakfast quickly and remember all the time that this is the *last* flight out!'

He went, tall and intimidating in a fresh khaki outfit similar to the one he had worn when she had first seen him. Lord! Was it only the day before yesterday? She felt as if she had fought him for years. Even lying down her legs were shaking. The door slammed behind him and Andrea shot out of bed, washing quickly and dressing with greater speed than she had shown in her whole life. The previous night seemed unreal now; her antagonism seemed equally unreal—all that stuck in her mind were his final words, 'the last flight out'.

She got out cereal and made toast and she was just pouring orange juice for two when he came back in. There was no mockery about him. He was all hard-headed engineer and boss-man and he ate breakfast without saying a word, his movements swift and economical.

'Get your things together,' he rasped as she stood and considered doing the dishes. 'That's the lorry pulling into the compound. You're on it.'

Andrea looked at him a little wildly, oddly reluctant to move. There was something about him that pulled her towards him in spite of her constant annoyance. It hung in the air, electric. It overwhelmed her fear, threatening to consume her.

The puzzle of it showed in her wide eyes and he stared down at her impatiently.

'You did hear what I said?' he enquired coolly and she nodded, her eyes anxious. There was utter turmoil inside her for no reason that she could understand, a strange longing. Her small even teeth bit against her lower lip, the same anxiety showing in her face.

He watched her intently, his jaw tightening, and then he muttered under his breath, reaching out and pulling her against him, catching her hair in one hand, twisting it around his fingers and pulling her head up. His hand was hard and uncompromising on her narrow waist as he tightened his hold on her hair, forcing her face to his and for a moment she met the power of his eyes before his mouth crushed her own remorselessly.

It was hungry, possessive, burning, but it was all over in a second, so quickly that she would have thought it imagination except that her lips were pulsing, her waist aching from the pressure of his strong fingers. She just stared into his eyes and he looked back at her expressionlessly.

'Go, Andrea!' He bit out the words but she stood there trembling.

'But you? What about——?'

'I'm a big boy,' he snapped. 'With a bit of luck I'll be right next to you when that plane takes off. If I'm not, I'm still capable of looking after myself. Stick to Harry all the time and don't risk charming anybody. There's going to be a certain amount of euphoria when that plane gets to Nairobi. You get out of there fast and back home to Kip and Auntie.'

He propelled her through the door just giving her time to scoop up her bag, and he surprised her by taking it from her as he hurried her across to the lorry. The men were all in the back, a little anxiety on all their faces, and Harry was with the driver. Kane tossed her up into the front with Harry and put her bag on her knee, his eyes ignoring her.

'Don't forget what I told you, Harry. Any trouble or any suspicion of trouble and that plane takes off. No waiting for me.'

'OK, Kane but I still think——'

'*I'll* think, you just go. Look after her. And get her out of here!' He shot one stern look at Andrea and then he was gone, the lorry pulling away slowly.

The rush had left her trembling even more. She was still dazed by what had happened in the trailer, unable to really believe it, and Harry looked at her with a wry smile.

'Bit of a handful, ain't he?'

'Overpowering,' she agreed tremulously, her face flustered. 'Will he get out?'

'Kane? Sure! Though with what he's having to do now he'll be mad enough to bang all their heads together and finish them off single-handed if they catch him.'

Andrea was just about to ask what Kane had to do when she had to make a hasty grab at her bag as the lorry bumped over the uneven road. It drew her attention to her possessions and she realised with a sort of slow horror that her shoulder-bag was still in Kane's trailer, her passport and money in it.

'Stop! Stop!' Her frantic shouts brought the lorry to a halt, the driver turning startled eyes on her, and Harry tried to catch her arm as she slid out to the ground.

'Come back! What are you doing?'

'I've left my passport behind. Go on, I'll come with Kane.'

'But what if he——?'

'Go on! He'll be furious if you don't. I'll come with him.'

She had no illusions about the shortage of time and few illusions about what Kane would say when she presented herself before him and begged for transport.

She began to run back to the clearing, thankful that it was still fairly cool, and after a second she heard the lorry pull away. Harry's concern for her was tinged with his awe of Kane and he had decided to obey the boss with no detours. She didn't know quite how she felt about that. She did know that she was very scared, little of the former abrasive Miss Forsythe left in her.

She could see a Land Rover standing in the middle of the clearing but there was no sign of Kane and she darted across to his trailer and grabbed her shoulder-bag, checking rather frantically that her passport was there. It was and she ran out, ready to get into the Land Rover and brazen it out when he came.

Fear almost choked her as she saw Kane already in the Land Rover and he was just pulling away.

'Kane! Kane!' She screamed his name at the top of her voice, waving frantically and running faster than she had ever run in her life. Terror at being left completely behind added adrenalin to her bloodstream and speed to her legs. If he didn't see her she would be here alone and everything he had said about the rebels crowded into her head.

Kane saw her as she tore up behind and he jammed on the brakes but as she came alongside he wasted no time in remonstrations although she could see that his fury was beyond belief. He simply set off again, curling one iron-strong arm around her waist and literally throwing her in beside him.

She went right over him and landed in the passenger seat, banging her head, his action so violent and furious that she ended up with her legs in the air, her skirt to her waist, but he shot off at top speed, never sparing her a glance.

'You uncouth, unfeeling monster!' Andrea scrambled upright, rubbing her head and turned on him furiously, yelling at the top of her voice, but his face stopped her onslaught.

'Shut up and start praying!' he snarled, his eyes on the road, his hands tight on the wheel. 'That trick of yours may very well be your last—mine too!'

'The lorry can't be too far ahead, so what are you so furious about? I forgot my passport——'

'You might not need one,' he grated. 'What the hell do you think we've been doing here? We spent the last two days setting charges along the line and I've just been back to detonate them. In a minute you're going to hear the biggest bang since creation. It may be the last thing you'll hear, thanks to your immaculate timing!'

Andrea tensed, her face paling, his speedy departure now explained, but a series of explosions, though loud, did nothing to impress her unduly and it was her turn to sneer.

'I think I'm made of sterner stuff than that,' she informed him with satisfaction.

'Are you?' he gritted, accelerating even more. 'That was the overture; the musical hasn't started yet.'

Andrea didn't have time to comment. A violent explosion ripped through the air, rocking the Land Rover and tearing branches off the trees. Stones began to fly over them and Kane pushed her head down as he drove furiously. The ground lifted, shook and subsided, dust covering them, trees rocking in their path which Kane had to dodge at great speed.

They were well along the track before the noise died and he made any move to drive reasonably and Andrea emerged breathless and shaken, very subdued.

'Was that the dam? Have you blown up the dam?' she asked shakily, her eyes filled with the same awe that everyone else had when they looked at Kane.

'I bloody well haven't!' he rasped, glaring at her as if she was a demented child. 'That dam is my baby. I'll be back!'

'But—but that big explosion?'

'We use explosives, lots of them, and Okasi wants them badly. He's not well equipped and our explosives may have made all the difference. We've blown the lot. Yesterday we set charges to the main dump. I went to detonate the lot when you left in the lorry.' He glanced at her angrily. 'I didn't set the timers for a stop to pick up hitch-hikers.'

'Will—will the rebels destroy the dam?' she asked, trying to take his mind off her latest crime.

'How?' he scoffed. 'Kick it down with their boots? When I build something it stays built. I've told you, I'll be back.' He was suddenly grimly silent and she bit her lip anxiously, her eyes warily on him.

'Damn you, Andrea,' he snapped out. 'Okasi will know already what I've done. That explosion will have been heard for miles and I know he's rushing here to get his hands on anything that goes bang. I hadn't figured on you being still here. If I had...'

'You were still here. What difference does it make?' she asked a little desperately.

'If we miss that plane you'll know the difference,' he warned darkly. 'Getting myself out is one thing, getting a woman out is yet another.'

'But we're not long behind them. How can we miss the plane?'

'You heard my orders to Harry. He'll go. He may not want to but he'll go. Today's flight is specially for us, laid on by the firm. We have no real idea where the rebels are and if they show up on that airfield Harry will give the order to take off because they're *my* orders. You didn't need any passport here and in Nairobi you could have gone to the British Embassy.'

'I—I'm sorry. I risked your life and probably my own. I'm sorry.' She gave a small laugh, partly compounded by nervous tension. 'I seem to be saying I'm sorry a great deal since I met you.'

'Let's hope for the best,' he said quietly. He glanced at her. 'Where's your travelling bag?'

'It—it's in the lorry.' She felt very foolish and inept; inside her too was a slowly growing fear of what they would meet at the airfield.

He nodded sagely.

'That figures. With you, it figures. I might have expected it.' He grimaced at her pale face. 'Oh, Andrea. I really should have come to meet you when Kip invited me. I would have known then what to expect. I could have sent Kip to Africa and gone to India myself. It would have been a whole lot safer all round if our paths had never crossed.'

She couldn't think of another thing to say except 'sorry' so she just looked down and said nothing at all. Kane was beside her, strong and reliable, but she was probably responsible for more than she had ever realised. If he was caught she would be responsible for that too. He had destroyed the explosives and she knew there would be no mercy for him if the rebels caught him.

It was only two days since she had come along this track but to Andrea it seemed like weeks ago. She had hoped and even expected that they would catch the lorry, but as they rounded every bend her hopes were dashed. There was no sign of it and she realised that at the sound of the explosion the lorry would have put on whatever speed it could. All they could hope for was that Harry would be able to wait for them.

They came within sight of the airfield and she noticed that the jungle came much closer to it than she had imagined. They were still partly under cover of the trees but she could see the aircraft on the tarmac, not a passenger plane of the size she had imagined in view of her flight here, but a much smaller plane. Kane had said that the firm had laid it on to get them out and she could see now what he had meant.

Andrea gave a great sigh of relief. Harry was waiting. Everything was going to be all right. Her spirits lifted on wings but there was a stillness about Kane that transmitted itself to her, making her turn her head sharply. He had slowed almost to a stop and she looked at him anxiously.

'Why are you——?'

'Quiet!' he snapped. 'Let me get a good look at the situation.' He was almost sniffing the air, his body alert, an animal watching about him that made the hair rise on the back of her hands. The tawny eyes swept the airfield and the surrounding area and he slowly let the Land Rover roll forward, but nothing about him relaxed.

Andrea looked too but she could see nothing unusual except that the plane was turning, taxiing forward to face the runway, getting ready to move as soon as they joined it. Why didn't Kane drive right up there? The gates were wide open! Her eyes never left the plane, hanging on to it as if she could keep it waiting by sheer will-power.

'Kane!' She grasped his arm in frustration, her fingers curling anxiously into the taut muscles, but it made no impression on him. Still they crawled forward with hardly any speed at all and Andrea's fingers bit into his skin, her teeth clenched in anxiety.

'Shh! Something's wrong.' His hand came over hers, pressing her fingers closer to his arm, making her feel better at the contact. 'It's too quiet. I made strict arrangements with Harry. He should have been at the door, the door open, but they're ready to run for it.'

A cold shiver raced down Andrea's spine but she had no time to really think. Suddenly there were shouts, shots, and she gave a little scream that was quickly stifled as soldiers ran out on to the airstrip, firing at the plane that seemed to leap into life. It picked up speed, racing away for take-off as more and more soldiers ran out from the shelter of the hangars. They were not the ones she had seen the day before yesterday. These were rough-looking, khaki-clad, ill-disciplined, firing wildly with little chance of hitting such a swiftly moving target.

In the noise and confusion, Kane reversed to the thicker trees and turned the Land Rover on to another track, a narrow rutted track that led deep into the jungle. They stopped for a moment, peering through the trees, and saw the plane lift off and turn north. It was safe.

Kane's powerful shoulders relaxed but Andrea was filled with horror. They were stranded here.

'They would have liked to get that plane, though Lord knows who they thought would fly it,' he murmured caustically.

Slowly and carefully he drove along the track. They could still hear wild, unnecessary shooting and she knew that under cover of this sound Kane was getting them as far away as possible.

'I made you miss the plane,' she whispered, and he gave her one swift look before going back to the tricky task of keeping their vehicle level.

'You didn't. Harry and the men could only just have made it by the look of things. There were more of Osaki's boys pouring out from the direction of the town as we left. I knew he would be heading for the dam with all speed but I didn't know he'd got quite that far. The sound of the explosives will have spurred them on. He'll be spitting mad,' Kane finished with grim satisfaction.

Andrea was filled with remorse all the same, astonished that he was taking it so calmly, although he wasn't the sort of man to grieve about something that was irretrievable.

They heard a dull explosion and Kane actually laughed outright, the first time she had ever seen him do that. It changed his face. The harshly handsome features came to life, his eyes glittering with ironic amusement.

'That's the lorry going up,' he explained when she looked at him questioningly. 'Harry and I made our plans very carefully.'

He meant *he* had! Kane wasn't about to leave a single thing for the rebels to use. She thought of the food in the camp.

'Maybe you should have blown the trailers up,' she suggested shakily.

'I did,' he assured her, looking grim again. 'No scruffy layabout is sleeping in my bunk and drinking my beer!'

Andrea had to turn her face away and smile at that. She had never met a more thorough, determined man. He just brushed opposition aside as if it didn't exist. She had never been even close to anyone like him; her life had been school and then university, boys she had known at school, men at university—all very predictable, all trained from boyhood to be civilised. Kane was different, a hot wind from the desert, a cold glitter from the icepack. He made his own rules. She should have been afraid of him, but she wasn't.

She clung to the side of the Land Rover as they bounced on the uneven track, her free hand pushing her ash-blonde hair away from her hot face.

'Scared?' His voice was deep and dark and he shot her a glittering sideways glance, those impossible eyes narrowed.

'Only as scared as you, I expect.'

He grinned to himself and she took that as a compliment, coming from Kane. She had the impression that he was almost enjoying this. If she hadn't been there he probably *would* have been enjoying it.

'Will we get out?' she asked quietly.

'Promises are not possible. The probability is that we will. It's only twenty miles to the border but it's a tough twenty miles and I don't know if he's got all his thugs together in one bunch or if they're spread out, apart from any support he's got along the way, so we avoid villages. I've got enough water and food here in the Land Rover. Your clothes are the main problem.'

He glanced at her short skirt, her long slender legs and bare arms.

'You're a very unprepared girl, Andrea. I've got to get something to cover up all that tender skin or you're going to be burned and scratched unmercifully.'

'I thought I'd be on the plane and back to civilisation,' she sighed. 'I'm sorry—again.'

'Not to worry. You're just one of the natural hazards of life. If the worst comes to the worst I'll put you in my pocket and run.'

'You'd get out faster without me,' she reminded him quietly.

'You're suggesting that I leave you here?' His voice was amused and she glanced across at his impassive face.

'I know you wouldn't.'

'So much faith in me, Miss Forsythe. You don't know me.'

'I do. You don't have to know somebody for years to really know them. Sometimes, you just—know somebody. I expect some people are married for years and don't really know each other at all because it's all built on false conceptions. It must be dreadful, living in close confines with a person who's really a stranger if you could see into his or her mind.'

'Philosophy? You're a little young to think such dark thoughts.' His voice was unexpectedly cool and Andrea glanced at him sharply.

'I was just musing.'

'An odd thing to muse about when you're up to your neck in danger.'

'We were talking about knowing you. One thought led to another, that's all.'

'You don't know me.'

It was definite and dismissive, almost contemptuous. She turned away, uneasily aware that she had stepped unknowingly into the dark edge of something she could not even guess at. She was back to pondering on the fact that some woman had hurt him, maybe married another man. It was a subject to steer clear of. She seemed to have developed a sixth sense as far as Kane was concerned, but it never quite stopped her tongue in time.

*   *   *

Some miles further on, Kane stopped the Land Rover and looked at the surrounding forest. For a long time he hadn't spoken and they had made as much speed as possible. Now he simply got out and walked round, looking up into the trees, looking back along the track. Andrea watched him anxiously. It was a particularly rough track, used only by people on foot, and few of them apparently. No vehicles had been along here; the only tyre tracks were their own.

He got back in, drove a little further and then stopped again.

'OK, Andrea. Out!'

She had no thought at all to disobey and she climbed out to stand at the side of the track, her eyes on him all the time.

'Get your bag,' he suggested evenly, 'and then stand at this side and wait. I'm not about to drive off laughing,' he added with sudden irritability as her eyes widened.

It was enough for her to really jump at obeying and he got back in as she stood and watched. This time, though, he turned into the trees, forcing the tough vehicle over a small bank and then climbing out. As she watched in astonishment he released the handbrake and pushed. She saw the muscles of his back bunch together under the khaki shirt, perspiration streaming down his face, and then the Land Rover toppled forward and disappeared. It was only then that she realised that as she had been getting her bag and moving to the side of the track Kane had been removing the food and water from the back, leaving it close by.

He stood tossing branches over the abandoned transport and then grunted in satisfaction.

'That should take some time to find.'

She didn't ask why he had wrecked their only form of getting out of here. If he had decided to do it then it must be the right thing.

'Will—will they follow us?'

His head shot up at the tremble of her voice and his eyes narrowed. For a moment he had forgotten about her, she was quite sure.

'I've pulled off on the only hard patch. We've left no tracks for the last few hundred yards,' he pointed out. 'As to following us, even they can see that a vehicle of some sort turned off on to this track from the airport. It might just never occur to them but you never know. The real danger was from the sound of the engine; it could be heard for miles. We've got all we could out of it. From now on we go on foot—we weren't making much speed with the Land Rover. We can cut across towards the border better if we walk.'

'Will they track us?'

'I doubt that's their line,' he informed her pithily. 'They might see an elephant if they fell over it but anything else will be sheer good luck or our stupidity. We're not going to be stupid.'

Andrea hoped he meant both of them and not just her. For someone who was supposed to be extremely intelligent she had gone a long way down since she had left England. She sighed and shouldered her bag, bending to pick up some of the supplies he had at the side of the track.

He took them deftly from her.

'I'll carry those. All you're required to do is keep upright. Follow me!'

That was how this had all begun, with those very words, she remembered. This time he hadn't called her 'you' in that nasty tone, but he was back to being as hard as nails, and she followed closely behind as he stepped off the track and moved into the trees.

It was terrible. The branches whipped at her and she was terrified that she would stand on a snake. She followed

Kane's steps exactly and she did not miss the fact that his eyes constantly scanned the trees ahead. She remembered Kip's excited tales about the things in the jungle and she was almost ready to scream with fright when half an hour later Kane suddenly stopped.

'Are you all right?'

He came very close to her, his voice low, and Andrea nodded, wiping the perspiration away that ran down her face and neck. She was thirsty, her legs hurt, but she wasn't about to complain. She knew that without her he would be going twice as fast. He looked at her steadily and nodded.

'You stay here and keep quite still and quiet. Just ahead there's a village where we bought supplies from time to time. They carried them up to the camp. I don't know where their allegiance is now, though, so I'll go in alone.'

'Why don't we just go round?' Her dark eyes were enormous, strained, and he glanced down at her legs, already scratched.

'We have to get some other clothes for you, some trousers and a long-sleeved shirt. I know this village and I know what they've got. Stay here until I come back for you.' His eyes went to her hair and he wrapped it around his hand, making it into a slender, glittering rope. 'Hold your hair like this. It's not a good idea to have it floating around your shoulders. I told you that yesterday.'

She couldn't help the shudder that ran through her and he closed her fingers around her hair.

'You'll be all right.' His thumb stroked her jawline softly and then he disappeared into the trees, leaving the supplies at her feet.

There had been no real need for him to tell her not to move. She dared not take even one step. The jungle was filled with sound, all of it alien to her. Birds called in the higher trees; strange noises seemed to fill the air lower down. Her eyes tried to see further than they could, her senses alert to danger, and she knew that for all her intelligence, for all her studies, she was helpless without Kane. Her self-confidence was undermined to such an extent that she was sure without him she would have walked straight into danger, in the jungle or at the hands of the rebels. She had always felt confident, resourceful, but it had all drained away and she relied on a man she hardly knew, her faith in him unbelievable considering how they had reacted to each other on sight.

He came back as silently as he had gone and by this time her nerves were so on edge that she opened her mouth to scream. His hand stopped that too quickly for any sound to escape.

'Calm down,' he ordered quietly against her ear. 'As far as I can see there's nobody there at all, the place is deserted, but you never know.'

'Maybe the rebels...' she began but he shook his head grimly.

'They've already been there and they're not likely to come back. The place has been ransacked but they didn't take everything. It looks as if the villagers just disappeared into the bush as they heard them coming. They'll not come back out until everything is safe.' He picked up the supplies and urged her onwards. 'Come on. Before too long you're going to have to rest.'

'I can manage.'

'Manage to do what?' he enquired caustically, and she was once again assured that she was a great big liability, her earlier feeling of companionship fading. She followed in silence and Kane said not one word more.

Outside the village he stopped and motioned her to his side, his hand coming to her arm. Together they listened. Apart from the jungle sounds that were by now patterned into Andrea's mind there was no sound at all, and Kane nodded his satisfaction.

'Now we do some looting.' He looked at her quizzically as she gasped in shock. 'Don't let your conscience
bother you. The whole place has been looted already. If
things return to normal I'll pay for your gear.'

They went quietly down the side of the only street and
Kane knew exactly where he wanted to be. In a few
seconds he was stepping in through the broken shutters
of a village shop and helping Andrea inside. They stood
in the gloomy interior, their eyes growing accustomed to
the light, and then he began to forage. He came up with
some khaki trousers and a matching shirt.

'Try these,' he muttered sardonically. 'The boy's
section. You look pretty much like an underdeveloped
youth.'

'How can there be a boy's section if they supplied
your camp?' she asked, embarrassed under his probing
stare. He might have scathingly compared her to an
underdeveloped youth, but his eyes were on the swell of
her breasts beneath her thin cotton shirt.

'They're not very good at sizes,' was his laconic reply.

To her astonishment he got her things that almost
fitted, including some boots.

'Get into these things while I keep watch at the door,'
he ordered. 'You've got about twenty seconds. Hanging
round here is really asking for trouble.'

He didn't need to point that out, she already knew
that, and Andrea was changed in less time than a quick-
change artist. He heard her soft call and came back in,
standing to look at her closely.

'I'll get you a cap for that hair,' he grunted, adding,
to her utter humiliation, 'Take off the bra.'

'I—I beg your pardon?' She flushed all over again
and glared at him.

'I said "take off the bra",' he repeated clearly. 'The
shirt's cotton, the bra is nylon. You can do without that
sort of thing in this heat.'

'How do you know that——?' she began unwisely and his dark brows rose ironically.

'You buy silk, Miss Forsythe? Pardon me.'

'Oh! Turn your back!' Andrea snapped, forgetting her utter dependence on him in her embarrassment. Instead he moved off while she struggled out of the offending garment, and when he came back he had a cap similiar to the ones she had seen on the soldiers who had attacked the plane. He proceeded to tuck her hair up under it while she watched in helpless fury.

'There!' he exclaimed softly. 'The perfect traveller's outfit. Give me your things,' he added with no mockery at all.

She handed him her skirt, blouse and, very reluctantly, her bra.

'The shoulder-bag in a minute,' he snapped, bundling her things inside a paper bag and then scraping a hole in the soft earthen floor behind the counter of the shop. To her astonishment he buried them and she was just sufficiently in charge of her brain to snatch her passport and money out of her bag before he grabbed that and buried it too. He stamped it all down and then kicked earth over it, looking very smug in her opinion.

'What do you think it is—vandalism?' he grated as she watched him in annoyance. She had been very fond of that skirt.

'It—it's pointless!' Andrea snapped back, sure it was his way of getting at her.

'Is it? I can't guarantee that Okasi's men will stay away from here. I have no intention of letting them know that a woman is somewhere in the jungle. If they knew that, they'd suddenly develop great skills in bush craft.'

In the heat, Andrea's skin went quite cold and he looked at her sardonically.

'Don't question my motives if you don't want the reasons,' he rasped. 'Let's get the hell out of here!'

CHAPTER FIVE

IT WAS more comfortable in this outfit, Andrea had to admit, and she walked with Kane down the single street, both of them keeping as close to the walls as possible. It was as well that they did because it meant that cover was close as they heard voices. After the silence of the village, only their own quiet voices in the dark shop, Andrea was stunned, rooted to the spot.

Kane was not. He acted with bewildering speed, his arm lashing round her waist as he almost lifted her round the corner of a hut. He did not give her the chance to remain silent. His hand clamped across her mouth tightly as his arm held her fast against him and they were both frozen into immobility as the sound of two voices came closer and closer.

As they approached, Kane edged her round the hut as far back as they could go and she saw two of the rebel soldiers hurrying down the street, talking to each other in loud voices, a touch of anxiety on their faces. They never looked round. They disappeared into the trees and as they went out of sight Kane almost raced her off in another direction.

'Will they come after us?' She was breathless and hot as they made the cover of the trees. 'Are they looking for us?'

'They're deserters,' he told her tightly, making her realise that he understood their language. 'They're nothing to worry us; they haven't even taken their guns. One thing it does tell us, though, is that the rest are behind them, somewhere over to the south. Okasi can't afford

77

deserters—his hold on things is too tenuous as it is.
Somebody will come after those two, and we don't want
to meet the hunting party.'

They were forced into even worse tracks now and Kane
told her to be careful where she was putting her feet.
She was grateful that he sheltered her as much as possible, his strong arm pushing aside branches for her to
move more easily, and she knew he would be miles ahead
if it were not for her. She badly wanted the rest he had
mentioned but she knew there was not much chance of
that now, and she stumbled on wearily, fear behind her
and the goal of the frontier far ahead.

From time to time he looked round, his eyes on her
strained face, but he went relentlessly on and Andrea
concentrated on counting her steps, anything to take her
mind off the weakness of her legs. Kane was uncon-
querable, his will-power capable of overcoming anything. She would not give in if he did not.

Before too long he stopped, listening intently as he
had done before, and she was too tired to question him
when he boosted her into a tree and climbed up beside
her. He pushed her higher until they were hidden by the
canopy of leaves, Kane settled firmly in the high fork
with Andrea pulled against him.

'What...?' She merely whispered but his arm tightened
painfully around her and his hand once again clamped
over her mouth. Her heart began to hammer madly, her
breathing tight and painful, and Kane slackened his grip,
his face against hers.

'Shh!' Kane's whisper was like the breeze in her ear
and she trembled against him, her eyes wide. Only then
did she see the soldiers along the path, their low, silent
run frightening her as she had never been frightened
before. A shudder ran through her and Kane held her
tightly as she watched them out of sight. How had he
known? He was like no man she had ever met before,

something almost inhuman about him. She raised her eyes, looking at him with fear still shadowed there, and he looked back at her steadily.

His hand slowly left her mouth but he frowned as she started to speak, shaking his head. Everything was now silent but he was still listening. After a while he relaxed, his cruel grip on her waist easing.

'We'll wait here for an hour,' he said quietly. 'There may be stragglers, and in any case you need a rest.'

'I can go on.'

'Gallant but untrue,' he murmured, his eyes on her flushed face, her damp hair. He gave her a drink and then pulled her against him again. 'Rest, Andrea.'

She wanted to and she tried to relax but she was uncomfortably aware that she was very close to Kane, resting between his strong thighs as he propped himself securely and held on to her.

'Rest,' he ordered, tightening her against him and giving her no choice. Her need to rest overcame her anxieties and she leaned softly back, her head against his chest, only too glad to obey, and he moved to accommodate her, his arm holding her safely, his shoulders relaxing against the giant bole of the tree.

'Will they come back?'

'No.'

'How can you tell?' she persisted, wondering if he was merely trying to ease her fears.

'They're searching for those deserters and they'll not search the same place twice. They've a pretty good idea where the two are going, I think. We stay here until you're rested and then we head for the border. It's not too far and I don't want to run into any of them at the last minute. The deserters would be forgotten. We're a much better prize for Okasi.'

Andrea didn't ask any more questions. Her mind finally told her that it was much better not to know. In

any case, she would obey Kane whatever he told her to
do. Ignorance was not quite bliss in this case but it was
as close to it as she was going to get. She fell asleep,
thinking as she did so that it was strange how safe she
felt. There were rebel soldiers close by, a long way to go
to safety, but Kane's arms were a safety by themselves.
She sighed and snuggled closer and as she drifted into
sleep she felt both his arms come around her.

Andrea awoke to find the air cooler, the light not so
intense, and she opened her eyes without stirring. Kane
was watching her closely, his expression unreadable.

'Did I sleep for a long time?'

He simply shook his head, saying nothing at all, his
eyes intent on her face, and she felt incapable of looking
away, of moving to sit up even. She was hypnotised by
those eyes; she had been since she had first seen him.
His lashes were thick, curled and very dark, framing the
golden eyes, making them look like jewels glittering in
the softer light. Andrea found her gaze searching his face,
memorising the hard planes, the strong mouth that curled
sardonically at the corners. His mouth was not sardonic
now, though, and he was intently searching her features
too, his eyes vibrant on her soft mouth.

'Your cap came off,' he told her quietly. 'I put it in
my pocket.'

She gulped a little and nodded. He was speaking
without thought, his mind on other things and one word,
one movement from her would break the spell. She knew
it with utmost certainty. She didn't want to break the
spell because it was there again, the wave of feeling, like
the lick of flames. In bewilderment she realised that she
wanted the flames to burn her and her lips trembled
helplessly.

She was behaving oddly, she knew, but she was so
acutely aware of the strength of the body close to hers

that emotion raced across her expressive face. For the first time in her life she really felt desire, a wave of feeling that made her swallow hard, her hands clenching against his shirt, bunching it in her fingers.

Kane's gaze narrowed at her expression and his lips twisted wryly as he read very accurately the message in the deep, fascinated darkness of her eyes. His strong hand closed around both of hers, pressing them closer to his chest, spreading out her fingers until she felt the thunder of his heartbeat, but his words were not encouraging.

'You drift from one problem to another. Poor Andrea.'

His voice was harsh, filled with cynicism, but his hand, moving to stroke her hair back, smoothing it to her head, was almost caressing. Without knowing it, her lips parted and his fingers slid into her hair and then beneath the weight of it as his hand closed on her nape. It was hard, warm, almost cruelly tight but she did not try to move. Lethargy gripped her limbs as his fingers massaged the base of her skull.

'Do you know what you're doing?' His voice was like dark silk and she shook her head slowly. She could see something that looked like self-contempt in his face but nothing could help her. Her eyelids felt heavy, lowering over her eyes, and he muttered angrily, a low growl of sound as his head bent to hers quickly, his lips closing over her own.

It was fierce, unexpected, but her lips parted again and his mouth opened over hers as he gripped her head tighter, lifting her face and deepening the kiss with a kind of subdued ferocity, demanding her submission. His mouth was probing, searching, drawing everything from her, the sort of kiss she had never even imagined, and he lifted her closer and closer.

She felt drained, every muscle relaxing, her breathing deep and slow, but her lips clung to his as they had so much wanted to do in the trailer that morning. Astonishing feelings raced through her body, pleasure searing her veins and twisting her up inside. She felt possessed, almost fainting with pleasure, her body a willing tool in his hands.

She had never known such physical strength, never felt such a turmoil of sexual recognition. She was completely at the mercy of a man who was little more than a stranger, but her body knew him, was eager, willing, and his mouth was claiming hers as if he knew his rights, hungrily, possessively devouring her.

Kane pulled her to his shoulder impatiently, leaving his hand free to caress the length of her neck. He tilted her head back, placing fiery kisses against her white throat, his hands arching her against him. She could feel heat racing through him, the same heat that she felt herself, but she was powerless to move, pliant and unresisting as his mouth came back to ravage hers. There was no gentleness. It was like a heated ritual but she obeyed the orders of his hands and lips, accepting every action.

His hand closed around her throat and then slid to her smooth shoulder inside the neck of her shirt, moving over her skin. Andrea felt her breasts tighten against the rough cotton and his fingers brushed over them, almost experimentally, and then slipped the buttons to her waist as his hand closed around one swollen mound, moulding it urgently.

He was fierce, almost cruel, but she moved closer, arching back and she couldn't stop her arm sliding around his neck, nor her fingers from tightening in the dark hair. As if he had been waiting for that, he jerked her closer, his teeth beginning to bite quickly against her lower lip as his fingers teased her, moving over the tight bud of her nipple until she twisted in frustration, a low moan escaping from her throat.

At the sound, he lifted his head and her lashes fluttered open. Eyes of brilliant topaz held hers, his hand still cradling her heavy breast, his thumb tracing erotic circles around the tender centre. They seemed to be locked in some vibrant sexual duel, staring deeply into each other's eyes, Kane's fingers caressing her urgently. She gave a sobbing sigh that was total submission and his eyes flared with excitement—triumph.

He looked down, his gaze moving over her breast and she felt no shame at all even though her body was throbbing under his touch. Nothing seemed astonishing. The electricity between them had finally arced. She felt she had known him for a long time, wanted this forever. He bent, his tongue stroking over her pained nipple just once, and she leapt in his arms, her body shuddering, her mind unable to believe it when she felt his fingers fastening her shirt, his hands smoothing her hair.

'We'd better get moving.'

His voice was so matter-of-fact that she could scarcely understand and her eyes were dazed on his composed face. What had happened to her? She had never allowed such intimacy with anyone before. Kisses had left her uninterested, bored, but now she was desperate for more, wanting those fierce hands back on her body. She was burning up inside, ready to go wherever he led, but he wasn't leading anywhere, his sole concern to get her out of Madembi.

'Have you been to sleep?' She was incapable of coherent thought, unable to sit up, still trapped in his arms, trite words springing to her lips in a sort of aimless defence.

He just shook his head, no emotion on his face at all. Even the self-contempt had gone; there was no anger, nothing. He was behind an iron wall of silence, shutting her out.

'I could have watched while you rested.' Her cheeks were hot, flushed, her eyes wild and puzzled.

'And done what had I slipped from my perch— grabbed my foot and held on?' he enquired with cool sarcasm, his eyes still holding hers steadily. 'Don't worry about me. I can sleep with my eyes open.'

He eased her away from him and began the descent, helping her down each part carefully but she was in no way in control of herself, although Kane had apparently dismissed what had happened altogether. Her feet didn't seem to be touching the ground as they made their way through the trees. Inside she was aching, a strange, lost, empty feeling raging through her. She had been given a glimpse of something she had never known, never dreamed of, and her eyes stayed on Kane as he moved with the power of an untamed creature through the darkening jungle, their shared, unexpected intimacy wiped from his mind. She was trembling, bereft, but he was utterly normal as if nothing had happened at all.

She should have been feeling shame, but she was not. In a daze, her mind tried to imagine what her reaction would have been if this had happened to her at home, in England, maybe at college. The answer frightened her. It would never have happened because she would never have allowed it. It could only happen with Kane. Plenty of men had kissed her before, had expected much from her, had been passionate, but she had felt only revulsion, repulsing them with embarrassment. Even the touch of Kane's fingertip on her lip had sent flames leaping through her. Her hand touched her swollen lips and she knew she would never be the same again, her eyes following him in an almost panic-stricken way. He felt nothing. He was just a hard, powerful man who would forget all about her the moment she was away from here.

He just drove her on, allowing no stopping. She fell several times but he simply hauled her to her feet and went on, his only concession a hard hand on her arm. Dusk began to overwhelm the jungle, the sounds that alarmed her more pronounced than ever, wild cries and unexpected rustlings that had her eyes wide with fear. Every dark tree seemed to hold danger and her breath was almost a sob in her throat, aching tiredness drowning all other feeling.

It was the sudden, added light that told her that the jungle had ended almost abruptly. They were in scrubland, her feet stumbling over the rough ground as she kept on going, wanting to put the terrors of the trees far behind her, thankful to be out in the light, however faded, and then Kane stopped, looking round and leading her to a hollow by a low tree.

'We stop here until it's really nightfall,' he informed her. 'The border is close but this area has no cover. It's better to cross in complete darkness.'

Andrea just stood there, looking at him. She was too tired to sink to the ground. Her hair was escaping from beneath the cap, fair tendrils curving along her neck, clinging to her wet skin. Her face was flushed and feverish looking and her eyes were heavy with exhaustion.

Kane rummaged in the bag he had been carrying and came up with a blanket which he spread on the ground.

'Sit here,' he ordered, helping her down. 'You can rest here now until it gets dark. We've almost made it. You can sleep on the blanket.'

'Why didn't you bring the camp-bed?' Andrea asked with weary humour. 'You seem to have plenty of other things in there.'

'I knew what I would have to do if I missed the plane,' he said briefly. 'The only thing I overlooked was you.'

He dived into the bag again and came up with some cream. 'Let's get a bit of this on those scratches while it's still light enough to see,' he said tightly. 'It will soothe them and it's antiseptic. You'll rest easier.'

She sat there as he applied the cream carefully, smoothing it in. When he came to her neck, she had to lift her face and his eyes flashed to hers just briefly before he continued his task with tightened lips.

'Go to sleep.' He pushed her down and flipped the end of the blanket over her.

'I'm too hot as it is,' she muttered but he paid no attention.

'You'll cool off rapidly. If you stay hot we'll move the blanket.'

Andrea curled up and she slept almost at once, but it was not a peaceful sleep. Her limbs were too tired, her mind too anxious and she tossed restlessly, moaning, her own voice finally waking her as the light was really beginning to go.

Kane was sitting up, watching the surrounding area, his arms across his knees.

'What can you see?' She struggled up but his voice was calm.

'Nothing. That's precisely what I want to see. Wherever the rebels are, they're not here. In a couple of hours we'll go.'

Her cap had come off again and she struggled to fix it as Kane turned to look at her.

'Leave it,' he suggested coolly. 'You're quite out of sight in this hollow and when we go it will be dark.' His eyes flashed over her face. 'Feel any better?'

'Not really.' She pushed her hair back with a weary hand and he nodded seriously.

'You were pretty restless. It's been a very tough experience for you.'

'I know I held you up,' she confessed. 'If I hadn't been here...'

'I would still have been at this precise point at this precise time, waiting for the light to go. You haven't held me up. What did you want me to do, leave you behind?'

'I deserved it.'

His eyes hardened dangerously. 'Are you trying for first prize as idiot of the year?'

His voice was harsh and she looked away, quite ready to have a small satisfying weep. He must have seen it in her face because he pushed her to the blanket again, his hand quite gentle in spite of his tone of voice.

'Finish your sleep.'

'I'm too uptight,' she muttered pitifully and he sighed like an adult who had reached the end of patience.

'Then just try to relax. Nothing is going to hurt you.' He pulled her into his arms and rested back with her and after a few anxious minutes she relaxed against him.

There was no sleeping, though. She felt wonderfully safe. She had wanted Kane to hold her, and even though he was only being unexpectedly kind she soaked up the pleasure of being in his strong arms. She sighed and curled towards him and he looked down at her, his hands stroking back her hair.

'I hope you realise that there's no future in this?' he muttered harshly.

'Did I ask for one? I know what's happening. You're just being kind. Not a thing you're used to, I expect. I—I know when you kissed me it was to—to drive me on. It had the desired effect. I made it, you see.'

The hand that had been slowly stroking her hair paused and then his fingers tightened in the silken strands.

'You're really clever, Miss Forsythe, to be able to work out my subtle motives,' he grated.

Andrea kept her eyes closed, surreptitiously trying to edge away but not gaining an inch. 'Oh, I am clever. I told you. Working out motives is fairly easy, especially with a man like you.'

'Really? What kind of man am I?'

'Hard. Ruthless. Powerful. You just sweep everything away that's in your path. If one thing doesn't work you turn to another, I expect, without any hesitation—hence the kiss.'

'You mean I'm a real bastard?' he asked, his voice low and menacing.

'No. I—I mean...'

'Care to tell me face to face?'

His fingers tightened again in her hair, giving a sharp tug, and she opened her eyes then, turning her face to look up at him. She had planned how she would look at him. It was to be sophisticated, amused, but it didn't work out like that. As soon as she looked into his tawny eyes her smile faded as feelings washed over her like the tide.

He watched her expression for a minute, his eyes narrowed to glittering points of light.

'If I thought you'd been looking at Sutherland like that...' he began threateningly and shock came to her face, pretence gone.

'I wasn't! He was hateful! I told you.'

'Then you *do* know how you're looking at me?' he asked softly.

She flushed anxiously. 'No. I was only g-glancing at you. I——'

'With pleading eyes.' He came up on one elbow and looked down at her. 'They're still pleading. Is this what you want? More Dutch courage?'

He bent, his lips brushing hers, sparks shooting between them at the first contact and he stiffened but it was too late, far too late. Her arms just seemed to float around his neck by themselves and with a groan he lowered himself over her, closing her in his arms completely, his lips possessive again, fierce, demanding.

His body was strong and heavy and he seemed to realise how fragile she was at the side of his strength because he eased away a little, moving his hand around her back, curving her to him, his lips never leaving hers.

She softened against him, tightening her arms around his neck, and his hand began to explore her slender body, her arched back, her legs, her smoothly curved thighs. His lips left hers to roam over her throat with less ferocity, his kisses now drowsy and slow, exciting her more, relaxing the tight feeling inside.

'Kane?' She whispered his name but his fingers traced her lips slowly as his own lips traced her throat.

'Shh!' He breathed against her skin and even that brought wild pleasure, the flutter of his breath enough to excite her further. She opened her eyes to see his dark head against her breasts, his hands possessing them, his fingers restless through the damp cotton of her shirt.

He slowly unfastened the buttons and ran his tongue over the swollen mounds one at a time, his hand sliding beneath her to lift her closer. It was an erotic ritual—necessity—and she felt a shudder race through him at her pliant acceptance. His hands were bruising her and instinctively she knew he was fighting to be gentle but wanting to take her fiercely with no waiting at all. The certain knowledge weakened her more, a sensual fragility that accepted her fate.

'You're so soft, so willing,' he muttered against her skin.

'Kane.' She breathed his name and the sound of her voice seemed to break the spell. He lifted his head and stared down at her.

'You don't know me!'

'I do.' Andrea refused to accept the sound of harsh contempt in his voice. She didn't know if it was directed at her or himself but he couldn't stop touching her. For a second his hands tightened on her as he watched the enchantment on her face and then he was sitting up, turning impatiently away, his eyes on the endless scrubland that was now quite dark.

'Let's go!'

His voice rapped out at her and when she just lay there staring at him with wide eyes he sat her up roughly, fastening her shirt, an act she seemed to be incapable of performing for herself.

'I must be losing my senses!' he gritted between his teeth. 'One hour and you'll be safe.'

'I'm safe with you,' she whispered shakily, and the golden eyes were turned on her ferociously.

'Oh, no, you're not, Andrea. I thought you were, but I was never more mistaken in my life. After giving Sutherland a black eye I should have gone to Harry and asked him to examine my head. Obviously I need speedy psychiatric aid!'

He jerked her to her feet and they set off for the border in the deepening darkness.

'What about the blanket?' Andrea whispered, too shaken to speak properly.

'Let's just forget about the blanket,' he snapped. 'Clearly blankets are dangerous things and we'd better not have one. If the rebels find it and your discarded cap the clues should send them mad!'

He urged her on over the uneven ground and when she finally fell heavily, in spite of his hand, he stooped and lifted her as if she weighed nothing at all and she was too tired to protest, weakened by her efforts to keep up with him and by his intense lovemaking.

Her silky head just fell to his shoulder and he held her close as he strode off. He *was* like Tarzan, after all, she mused light-headedly. She wanted to turn her face into his neck, kiss the strong column of it, but he was wildly angry with himself although he had calmed a little by now.

'Are there any lions?' She was quite beyond caring, but it came into her mind and it was as well to know.

'No. It's a good thing you're still at university. Your knowledge has astonishing gaps in it.' He was mocking but his voice was still harsh and Andrea felt a wave of annoyance in spite of her exhaustion. He had no right to kiss her like that and then just go back to his normal character.

'My subject is history.'

'I'd love to see you at it. Do you look all prim with horn-rimmed specs?'

'How can you joke when we're in such danger? If it was a joke. And you can put me down!' she snapped shakily.

His arms tightened round her. 'Brave words. Your legs have finally given out, my pet. We're almost there. I can see the border. Better to carry you than drag you across by your hair.'

She lifted her head but it was so much effort that she rested back again. She hadn't the slightest doubt that he could carry her for hours.

'Why did you call me that?' She knew she must be delirious to ask such a stupid question.

'You're a weird child. I keep remembering that,' he growled.

'I'm twenty-four and you didn't treat me like a child when——'

'Shut up, Andrea!'

Suddenly he was angry again, not mocking any more, and she knew that he despised himself for kissing her, for touching her, and she remembered the look on his face when she had said he would make an abominable husband. There was somebody he loved. Somebody who had hurt him. She knew it instinctively and her heart felt unbearably heavy. How could anyone resist him? Andrea knew already that she couldn't. It was tiredness, tiredness and fear. Hadn't she fought him on sight? Didn't she hate great big rough men? It would be all right tomorrow.

They slipped across the border in the darkness. Kane seemed to know every path, every bush. He had not spoken at all except to issue quiet orders after he had allowed her to walk again and Andrea was too tired and distressed to do anything other than obey instantly. Her exhaustion had even drowned out her desire. A welcome numbness had spread all over her.

The township was unlit, unpaved, typical of the area, but there was an hotel of sorts, a small place that had once been painted white but had long ago given up any pretence of grandeur. It was close to a market that even at this hour was bustling and alive, filled with brightly clothed women, their long dresses sweeping the dusty ground as they haggled about prices. The scene was lit by naked light bulbs strung along the stalls and everyone was too busily engaged to take any notice of them as they went into the hotel.

They were ignored there too, given two rooms by a bored-looking clerk who yawned into their faces as they collected their keys and then Kane was helping her up the stairs to her room, not uttering one word.

He glanced wryly at the interior as he opened her door, his lips twisting with distaste.

'Well, it's not much but it's better than nothing,' he commented. 'I'm next door. Get a shower and then fall into bed.' He glanced at her. 'Are you hungry?'

Andrea just shook her fair head. She was too exhausted to be hungry and even if she had been she didn't fancy the sort of food she would be offered here. She collapsed on to a chair.

'When can I expect to get out of here and back to Nairobi?' she asked weakly, her eyes closing.

'Tomorrow. I'll get transport in the morning and we'll move first thing. Don't go to sleep there,' he added sharply as her head began to sink lower. 'Get under the shower and get those scratches washed.' She nodded, obedience to Kane drilled into her, but she made no move.

'Andrea!' She sat up straight at his impatient growl and he snapped at her. 'I know you're all in, but make this one last effort. I'll be back to see that you have!'

'Oh, stop bullying me!' She stood, swaying dizzily. 'It's all you ever do!'

'Not quite,' he bit out acidly. He walked out and she knew she had better get moving or she would be incapable of moving at all. She also knew that Kane would not kiss her ever again. They were back in civilisation of a sort, and his hard mind would control any urges he had as far as she was concerned. That was what they were, after all, primitive urges from a primitive man. She tried to tell herself that she too felt nothing other than that, but her mind mocked her silently.

It was stiflingly hot, even so late into the night, and no wonder, she thought as she saw that the shutters were tightly closed. She walked across and threw them open, looking for a minute at the moonlit night. The moon wasn't red tonight. It was a great orb of white gold, romantic if you were up to it. She could still hear the market round at the front of the hotel and she supposed that this had to be civilisation of a sort. Anyhow, Kane expected there to be a shower.

Andrea sat down on a tatty settee and began to take off her boots. Her passport was curled and sticky against her waist and her roll of notes was actually wet. She put both items on the settee. What a place! The cool halls of Oxford came into her mind and she sighed wearily, jumping with alarm as a large insect landed beside her.

'Ugh!' It was big, rearing itself up, looking right at her. She swiped at it with her passport and it flew off, only to circle and come back to the exact place.

'Go away!' Her voice raised hysterically as she swiped at it again with exactly the same result but this time it came back with what she took to be an angry insistence. It was reared up higher—glaring at her. She began to scream, her self-control utterly gone.

CHAPTER SIX

'ANDREA! What the hell...?' Kane came crashing into the room but she couldn't look away from the beast, couldn't stop screaming, and he strode forward and shook her hard before knocking the intruder with his flat hand, right out of the window.

He slammed the shutters and locked them into place, storming back to glare down at her, as she sobbed, still on the edge of hysterics.

'It was only a praying mantis, for heaven's sake! Why did you open the shutters? You want every villain in town up here?'

'I—I was h-hot!' she sobbed, tears running down her exhausted face.

'There's a fan right over your head,' he rasped, striding forward and switching it on. Instantly cool air began to circulate as the blades rotated and she looked at him reproachfully, her dark eyes filled with tears.

'I never noticed. I was too *tired*!'

He walked back and looked down at her, his face rueful, his annoyance gone.

'My fault. I should have done it for you. Another sin.'

She shuddered and he slowly pulled her into his arms, stroking her hair back and resting his chin against her head. 'Calm down now or you'll never sleep. It was only a harmless creature—like me.'

'I knew what it was,' she informed him in a choked voice, sobs still not too far off. 'And it's not harmless. They have disgusting habits. I know all about them!'

He gathered her closer. He was laughing softly. She could *feel* him laughing at her and it infuriated her, or at least it would have done if she hadn't been so tired.

'I'm not embarrassed that I screamed and shouted,' she told him fiercely, her face buried against his chest. 'Women don't like things like that. It's not their nature in the first place and, in the second place, I never pretended to be brave.'

'You are, though,' he said softly, tilting her face and looking down at her.

'I am?' A tear escaped and ran down her cheek and he wiped it away.

'You are,' he assured her. 'You faced the fact that the plane had left us as coolly as any of the men would have done and you came through the journey like a hardened explorer.'

'I was scared all the time,' she confessed, looking up, drowning in his eyes.

'But you kept quiet about it. Everybody gets scared. You kept quiet and kept going. That's brave.'

He went on looking down at her and her legs felt as if they would collapse. How did he manage to have this effect on her? She wasn't tired at all now. Everything in her had come to wild, singing life. Her eyes seemed to be unable to leave his hard lips and he suddenly put her away, a tight frown on his face.

'The shower, Andrea,' he reminded her, stepping away and moving to the door.

'I—I haven't got any clean clothes,' she stammered the words out, ashamed of her feelings and he nodded.

'Neither have I. I'll see what I can get before the market closes. I hope you don't mind a pink sari?'

She felt terrible. She had wanted him to kiss her, invited it shamelessly, but he had wanted no such thing; the very thought of it had annoyed him. Maybe he had only been encouraging her before because she was brave?

She blushed when she thought of his hands and searching fingers on her breast, his lips fiercely ravaging hers. Who was she fooling? He had felt a man's sudden desire and she had been right there, sleeping in his arms and later very obviously willing to be anything he wanted. Her standards were falling pretty low if she was then going to beg for it all over again.

She went off to the shower and was pleasantly surprised to find it clean, a couple of large white towels there that actually looked new, soap and shampoo and a comb in a sealed plastic container. Maybe they were expecting to be taken over by a chain of international hotels? She giggled madly and stepped under the stinging water.

It removed the hysteria and the burst of euphoria and when she stepped back into the bedroom, her brief panties washed out and drying in the bathroom, her body covered to the shoulders by the second of the towels, Andrea felt pretty sorry for herself. She was the owner of a sweaty passport, a roll of soggy money and a pair of panties. Kane had even buried her sandals. She combed out the tangles in her hair and stared forlornly at her image in the mirror. Even her nose looked suspiciously red. As a female knight-errant she was a dead loss.

Her shattered self-confidence was still showing on her face as Kane knocked briefly at the door and just walked right in. It was somehow typical of the way things were and she stared at him solemnly. She was devastated to find how much she wanted him, how much it hurt that he could reject her at will.

'No need to look so dejected,' he commented. 'I've had a successful shopping spree.' He held up a rather brightly coloured cotton dress. 'I'm afraid it was child-size—you being so minute. In any case, when women mature here they take to the great big sweeping dresses.

One of those would make a tent for you, complete with cooking quarters.'

She couldn't see why he found all this so funny, why he should find it so easy to slip back into his ironic attitude, and she frowned at the dress as he tossed it to the back of a chair.

'It might cling a bit,' he continued drily, 'but I've only got to get you to the plane.' What on earth did he mean by that? Andrea stared at him in pitiful hostility. 'About the—er—smalls. I couldn't get anything small enough.'

'They'll dry by morning.' Andrea spoke briskly to cover her embarrassment and growing despair. 'I've washed them and . . . What about you?' she asked, hurriedly changing the subject.

'Ah!' He leaned against the door-frame, his eyes gleaming at her. 'The clerk at the desk assures me that he can get my gear laundered by morning. I pointed out the inadvisability of failure.'

'I'm surrpised he even answered you,' Andrea muttered, remembering how many times the man had yawned into her face.

'He didn't fancy a good shaking,' Kane assured her drily.

'I know how he feels.'

'Do you? I haven't shaken you.'

'You *did*! When that hideous creature——'

'Ah, well, that was a medical necessity. You were spiralling into hysteria.'

She looked down at her bare feet, feeling very vulnerable again, realising all at once that she was standing here exchanging back-chat with a powerful male when all that covered her was a towel, her body inside it aching for his touch.

'I haven't got any shoes.'

'I quite forgot.' He tossed a pair of rubber flip-flops to the floor and she stared at them resentfully.

'Thank you. I'll look wonderful! They'll clear the way for me, get their cameras clicking!' she snapped.

'I can get your jungle gear laundered,' Kane offered. 'It was a bit rough on your delicate skin, though,' he added, looking at her bare arms. 'How are the scratches?'

He sauntered over and stood looking down at her and she looked at her toes hastily, curling them up in anxiety.

'They're all right. I'll survive the next few days.' He didn't answer and she looked up, ashamed to find that tears glazed her eyes. She felt drained again, tired, confused.

'Andrea,' he murmured. 'A silky name for a silky girl.' He ran his fingers through her newly washed hair. 'Do you know that the colour of this fascinates me? I've got to ask the question. Is it real?'

'Kip's fair,' she muttered desperately, her hands clenching into the towel.

'Reasonably so,' he agreed. 'Kip's hair doesn't look as if it's been washed in moonbeams, though.'

'I've always been fairer than Kip,' she said quickly, looking frantically away. 'It's quite real. Everything about me is real,' she added with a shaky attempt to lighten the atmosphere.

'Oh, I know that.' His voice was smokily dark, the words murmured from deep in his throat, and she glanced up, almost frightened, colour flooding her face as his hands came to her bare shoulders.

His eyes locked with hers and then he reached for her. She just had time to gasp his name and she was tightly in his arms, being almost lifted off her feet, his mouth ruthlessly on hers again with the same fiery hunger. It wasn't any use resisting and, in any case, she couldn't, she didn't want to. His lips seemed to be something she needed wildly, something she had been missing all her life. Her arms wound around his neck and she felt her feet actually leave the floor as he tightened her against him.

This time, standing against him, things seemed so much more erotic, and the towel was less barrier than her shirt had been. It was slipping. She could feel it move but she didn't seem to care. All modesty and anxiety had gone as soon as his lips touched hers. There was just a searing heat, a hunger, wild and soaring, consuming her. The air around them seemed to be thick with emotion like a tidal wave of heat.

His hand slid inside the towel, ruthlessly closing over her breast, and as she arched against him, her arms tightening around his neck, he growled deep in his throat, pulling the towel free and dropping it to the floor, his hands closing fiercely around her.

'I can't keep my hands off you,' he muttered angrily. 'I want to touch you all over.'

She knew she should be panicking, pulling free, but her body seemed to be boneless, melted completely, glowing under his touch. His breathing was harsh and unsteady, his hands running over her, searching her quivering skin with a kind of intent desperation. He cupped her taut bottom, holding her against him with one hand as his other twisted in her hair, pulling her head back, his mouth plundering hers remorselessly.

She had never before been naked in a man's arms. She was wanton, her mind told her, shameless, but her body moulded itself to him and he slid her to the floor, his hands tight on her hips, holding her against him, his mouth buried against her throat. She could feel him throbbing with desire, his breath rasping harshly, restraint gone, and she knew she would not make one move to save herself.

His head bent to her breast, his teeth nipping painfully, making her cry out before he drew her aching flesh into the soothing heat of his mouth. She arched her back, his lips against her body until she felt faint, fire tearing through her.

He lifted her as if she were gossamer and it was only then that she realised she was sobbing his name desperately, clinging to him so much that when he dropped her to the bed he had to unlock her arms from his neck. Kane kept her hand tightly in his and bit sensuously at the mound of her thumb, his eyes burning possessively. He looked down at her, his glance sweeping over her like liquid fire, and then he drew the sheet over her and straightened up.

'Sleep, Andrea,' he ordered harshly.

'With you?' Her face was rose-flushed, her pale hair a silken swathe over the pillow and his eyes lingered on it, on her bruised lips.

'No!' The flush of desire heightened his cheekbones but his eyes were uncompromising.

'I want to.' She looked up at him, knowing she was shameless but unable to stop the truth from falling from her lips.

'In spite of my inability to control my base instincts, I don't want an affair with you, Andrea. When I told you that you needed a man I didn't mean me,' he rasped. His eyes were narrowed on her face, the lids heavy, shuttering his gaze. 'Go to sleep. Tomorrow I'll get you out of here.'

And out of his life, out of his hair, as he had said before, Andrea recalled as he left the room, dropping the latch and leaving her in the lamplight. She was in a turmoil inside, aching, frantic, and Kane had recovered as speedily as before. She had not had one single doubt that he wanted her. Why had he stopped? Because she was Kip's sister? Because of that woman who...? Shame flooded through her as she remembered her body's abandonment to him. She could never have stopped, hadn't wanted to. If he came back now...!

She put her clenched fist to her mouth and closed her eyes, a wave of panic washing over her when she realised that she would never be the same again. He had said he did not want an affair with her. Was he like that with other women, so fierce, so passionate? To her it was a magical commitment. Nobody else would ever kiss her like that; her body would never respond so wildly, would never recognise another man. She felt her life had been changed, shattered, any innocence gone. It was a long time before she calmed enough to sleep and even then she awoke many times, her body restless with remembered need as if it craved only one man and knew it.

Breakfast was delivered to her room, tea and golden toast with marmalade, and when she looked surprised she was told that the *bwana* had ordered it to be brought here. Andrea was filled with gloom, wondering how she was going to face Kane today. He had made sure she was fed in her room so that he would see less of her, and she was still hot with the guilty thought that she had brought about all that had happened.

Her mind reasserted itself. She had done nothing of the sort. When she was close Kane just reached for her fiercely as if he had every right to, as if he couldn't help it, even though he obviously resented it. She would have to face him and make him see that she didn't care.

She was dressed when he came for her, the cotton dress clinging as he had surmised. It wasn't too bad. Her figure was slender enough to take it, but she had the nasty feeling that anyone would be able to see through it and she knew exactly where her bra was—buried beneath a shop floor!

Andrea had herself under tight control. She had not shrugged off her shame about last night, and the way Kane had pointedly had her breakfast served in her room was a reprimand. She opened the door when he knocked and stood stiffly waiting.

'Ready?' He made no move to come in and she gathered up her few things.

'Yes.' She lifted her head proudly only to find his eyes roaming over her, lingering on the swell of her breasts, convincing her that she had been perfectly right about this dress. She flushed wildly as his gaze lifted to hers. His lips looked sensuous, his eyes heavy-lidded, and a muscle twitched suddenly at the corner of his mouth. He was gleamingly clean, his khaki gear very freshly laundered, and Andrea looked away quickly as she found her eyes roaming over him of their own volition.

'I take it that you got your breakfast?' he murmured, his eyes going to her tray.

'Yes, thank you. It was kind of you to have it sent up to me.'

'Kind?' he queried sardonically. 'I did have some idea of how that dress would look. I had to go out to get us some transport and I didn't want you eating with the motley crew who seem to be staying here.'

She looked up quickly.

'So that was why...'

'That was why—what?' he asked quizzically, his dark brows raised, only puzzlement on his face. 'I might add that I went into the kitchen to oversee the making of it,' he added ironically, 'knowing as I do that you're a delicate girl.'

'Oh!' Her eyes were dark and glowing, foolish with happiness. 'Weren't they annoyed?'

His lips twisted wryly as he stood looking at her. 'I never asked them. I just made sure it was clean. If the interrogation is over, we'll go.'

He had commandeered a decrepit-looking taxi with an equally decrepit driver but it got them to the small airfield a few miles from town and there the name Mallory-Carter got them a charter flight to Nairobi. The pilot was American, he knew Kane in any case and after one brief searching look at Andrea he settled to his task, Kane sitting by him talking while Andrea sat behind trying to be fearless and watching Kane surreptitiously because she knew that Nairobi would be the last time she would ever see him.

The thought seemed to fill her with dread. In such a short time he had become her whole world, and she realised with shame that she had simply taken his word about Kip and thought very little about her beloved brother since. It was impossible to think about anything or anyone when Kane was near.

She forced her mind back to Oxford, making herself remember her real life. She would soon be there, back to her work, Africa forgotten. Kane would fade into the very back of her mind eventually and she would not even be able to remember his face. She would get over it. They said that everyone did eventually, even if it was someone you—loved.

'All right?'

He turned in his seat and spoke to her over the noise of the engine and she nodded, her gaze helplessly locked with his. For a moment he didn't turn away; his eyes lingered on her face, on her shining hair as the sunlight caught the pale, glittering strands. A faint colour came up along his cheekbones and his eyes narrowed, burning amber in the light of the sun.

'Not long now.' He turned away abruptly and she realised she had been holding her breath, willing him to want her. She blushed painfully, glad he was no longer looking, feeling like a schoolgirl, swamped by raw masculinity. She *would* remember his face. It was burned into her mind, into her body. A wonderful thing had happened to her but it was quite useless after all, merely an enchantment, unreal.

*   *   *

FORBIDDEN ENCHANTMENT 105

It was a relief to feel the breath of sanity that Nairobi brought, to see people going about their daily affairs, offices open, good shops; and there was nothing decrepit about the taxi that sped along the road to the hotel.

'Will everyone be there?' Andrea asked as they flashed along the main thoroughfare.

'The boys from the dam? No. They're staying across town where they can get a bit of "entertainment",' Kane said sardonically. 'You really wouldn't like it there. I'm afraid the adventure is over for you.'

Andrea flushed under his ironic gaze. She knew what he meant by entertainment. She wondered if he stayed there normally, wherever it was? The thought filled her with a wild desire to lash out at him and his final remark fuelled the need to hurt back. Was that what all the love-making had been—part of her adventure?

'I was merely worrying about my luggage,' she assured him coldly. 'I can hardly travel home like this and wherever they are I assume that Harry has my belongings.'

'I'll get them as soon as I've got you settled,' Kane informed her shortly, the amused derision dying.

'I can get myself settled.' She was uptight, ready to fight, and he knew it.

'You fancy walking in and demanding a room looking like that?' he drawled. 'You'd have a stream of waiters following you, all goggle-eyed.'

'It was you who got the damned dress!' Andrea snapped. 'And it was you who——'

'Buried your bra? Go on, say it, fear nothing. That being the case, I feel responsible for the safety of your person until you're right back in your own clothes and your normal frame of mind.'

'There's nothing wrong with my frame of mind!' Andrea hissed, perfectly sure that the taxi driver was leaning back and listening. Before long he would be stopping to see what was wrong with her dress. She folded her arms across in front of her and Kane laughed softly, amusement back in his voice.

'Oh, Andrea! It's not really that obvious. Nobody is going to look further than your beautiful face and your glorious hair.'

That shook her. Did he really think she was beautiful, that she had glorious hair? She subsided, defeated as usual in any battle with Kane, and she found herself walking behind him like a squaw as he strode into the best hotel and signed them both in. Of course he was known here too! In his fresh khaki and with his striking tan he looked like someone from a safari film. Heads turned as he strode in—women's heads—and Andrea felt hopelessly inadequate, like his servant, trailing behind. She felt that she should be carrying bundles on her head, calling him 'master' and ducking her head when he looked at her. It irritated her vastly.

He wasn't the only one in khaki either. She was fascinated out of her seething thoughts when a man came up to speak to him, pouncing on him and wringing his hand.

'Kane Mallory! It must be three years...?'

'Hello, Roy.' Kane was grinning at him as they slapped each other on the back, both bronzed and tall, two giants together. The newcomer was tanned to an even deeper brown than Kane, a wide-brimmed hat pushed rakishly to the back of his head. It had a thin leopardskin band round it and she found herself looking into the piercing blue eyes of a man who lived almost exclusively out of doors. A hunter.

'Roy is a game warden,' Kane introduced, almost as if he could read her mind. 'He's a crack shot. He can hit a playing card even when it's out of sight,' he joked.

'Especially when drunk,' Roy added with a wide grin. His eyes never left Andrea's face. 'What—is—this?' he enquired with a close look at Kane.

'Andrea Forsythe,' Kane said, adding quickly, 'Kip Forsythe's sister. We've just been getting out of Madembi together.'

'Have you, by heavens?' His attention was back with Kane at once. 'I thought you'd come in on the company plane?'

'We missed it,' Kane informed him wryly, and Roy's looks were very different as his eyes fell once more on Andrea.

'Her too? There's a story in this. It's worth a celebration dinner.'

'She's only got this evening,' Kane said firmly. 'We'll join you here at eight if you like. First, I have to rescue her clothes.'

'Ah! Yes!' Roy murmured, his eyes running over her with almost open speculation, and Andrea blushed furiously as Kane led her to the lift. He didn't quite take her hand and shoo her along but it was all there underneath. She bottled her annoyance in until he showed her into her room and then she turned on him.

'Did you have to bring his attention to my dress?' she seethed, her eyes flashing sparks.

'No. Surely you noticed his attention wandering there of its own accord? I thought I did very well to divert him with the bit about our adventure. Roy is quite a man for the ladies.'

'I don't want to dine with him or anyone else,' Andrea snapped spitefully, turning away. She knew perfectly well that she didn't want any of those women looking at Kane but nothing would have made her admit it, even to herself. 'I'll go to bed early and get the first flight out.'

'You'll have dinner with me,' he announced in a hard voice, walking across and taking her arms in an equally hard grip. 'If you think I'm letting you eat in your room . . .'

'You did this morning,' Andrea defied, trying to pull away.

'I explained that, I think,' he rasped, his eyes narrowing dangerously. 'I've also explained why you're in this hotel instead of the one with the men. I expect the courtesy of your company at dinner. Roy Bennet will make a welcome addition. He can flirt with you and no harm done because you'll be long gone tomorrow. The last thing I want is a cosy candlelit meal with you.'

He swung round and walked out of the room and Andrea found her eyes filling with tears. She dashed them away impatiently. It was quite ridiculous. It was merely sexual attraction, nothing to be pleased about, but why did his words cause her so much distress? He had more sense than she had, after all. He recognised it for what it was and he wasn't about to be romantic now. Her own thoughts distressed her. She had never had much time for moonstruck people, men or women.

When he came back with her bag afterwards she accepted it coolly and he didn't linger to talk to her. He assumed that with sensible outfits and in a civilised place she was capable of taking care of herself, no longer enthralled by a man she had recognised on sight as being uncivilised.

She was back to normal. With a shower and her own clothes back on she looked at herself in the mirror and felt nothing but annoyance at Kane Mallory. So he insisted on dinner? He didn't really know her. She would let him see what she was really like. Thus far he had seen her fall from a lorry and be surrounded by men, seen her reduced to washing at a trailer sink, seen her in khaki trousers and shirt dragged across the jungle and finally in a dress that had been an embarrassment. She wondered darkly if he had done that last on purpose to reduce her to a pitiful slave.

There was a small compartment at the bottom of her bag and she fished about inside and came up with her return ticket to England. She also came up with her credit card. Aunt Maureen had insisted that she separate her things, in case of thieves, a subject very close to her aunt's heart, thieves according to her being round every corner. Now Andrea looked at her credit card with satisfaction and later marched out of the hotel, heading for the very best shops. Kane could see the cool Miss Forsythe, the one they saw at lectures but somewhat glamorised. She would not be enchanted. He was after all merely a rough, unkind man.

She was ready when he called for her at eight. Whether he had called for her earlier when she had been out she did not know but she doubted it. She glanced quickly at herself before opening the door. Her afternoon had been well spent, her credit card used freely; she would worry about that later.

The silky black dress had a wide swinging skirt that came to just below her knees. The bodice clung to her breasts, leaving her back bare and plunging low at the front. Her hair was pale ice against it, piled on her head and pinned skilfully in a soft swirl that skimmed her forehead. She wore no jewellery whatever except a small silver chain that matched her high-heeled silver sandals and bag. She looked cold, sure of herself, more than twenty-four and quite untouchable. Kane would see that her reaction to him had been all in the heat of the moment, a shared danger with nothing but that. She quickly dabbed on perfume and went to open the door.

Kane was leaning elegantly against the door-frame, a Kane she had never seen before, the boss of the dam no longer there. In his place was the wealthy Canadian

businessman who wielded great power, Kane Mallory of
Mallory-Carter.

They just looked at each other in silence because she
was as taken aback as he. Kane looked impossibly
handsome in a grey suit, his matching grey tie against a
white shirt. She had never seen him dressed up before
and her act almost slipped but she managed a tight smile
as she stepped out to join him.

His eyes skimmed over her, down the length of her
legs, along the graceful curve of her neck and then
lingered on her breasts, tight against the bodice of the
black dress.

'The Little Ballerina,' he murmured softly. 'So that's
how you look.'

'It wouldn't have been suitable to arrive at the site like
this,' Andrea pointed out coolly.

'Or safe,' he rejoined silkily, taking her arm and
moving towards the lift. 'Although, on second thoughts,
it might have saved trouble. The men would probably
have realised that you were far above them.'

Something in his voice made her feel that he knew
quite well what she was doing and why she was doing it
but when she glanced at him he was not looking at her
at all; his face was tight with what appeared to be anger
and she was greatly relieved. Better to have him angry.
She wasn't sure of her ability to cope with anything else.

Roy Bennet was also dressed for the occasion, although
nothing would ever be able to remove the look of the
wilds from his face and his penetrating eyes.

'My dear, you're beautiful,' he commented graciously,
his blue eyes twinkling. 'So much more lovely than Kip.'

'I think Kip is the most handsome man in the world,'
Andrea smiled, relaxing a little when she saw that Kane
had been called away to speak to other people. One of
the women put her hand caressingly on his sleeve and

he was smiling down at her. Andrea looked away fast and turned all her charm on Roy.

'Do you really have to leave tomorrow?' he asked softly. 'Can't you stay on a few days? After getting out of that place you should take a rest. You're too slender.'

'I've got to get back,' Andrea told him quickly with a small smile. 'I'd love to stay but it's impossible.'

'Maybe I'll persuade you before the evening is over,' he murmured suggestively. His eyes were intent on her skin, on the rise of her breasts, and she felt a moment of panic, wanting to turn round and call to Kane. When Kane looked at her she melted, but she felt only distaste at the thought of what this man was thinking.

'Kane will be taking me to the airport tomorrow,' she said firmly, hiding behind Kane's size and temper. 'He feels responsible for me,' she added as an extra threat. She had been intending to flirt with this man, to make Kane see that her feelings for him were not at all special, but now she wanted him back with a deep ache that carried its own message to her brain.

'Lucky devil.' Roy's mouth twisted wryly. 'If there's nothing else, you can give me some information, then. Did you have a tough time getting out?' He glanced a little nervously towards Kane. 'Kane never talks about things. He's a secretive devil. Did he have to kill anybody?'

'No!' Andrea laughed, relieved to be off the subject of herself and amused by his bloodthirsty attention. 'We hid and we walked and walked. Nothing more.'

'Nothing more? With Kane Mallory? He's all ferocity. You've got to be hiding something. This is a conspiracy. *He* wouldn't tell me either.'

'What conspiracy?' Kane asked, joining them and sitting opposite.

'She says nothing happened on the way out of Madembi.'

Kane's eyes held Andrea's for a second. 'Nothing worth speaking of,' he murmured. 'We simply walked out.'

'What about the dam?' Roy's eyes flashed to Andrea's suddenly pale face, the speculation back in his eyes, but if Kane noticed he preferred to ignore it.

'I blew the lot, all except the dam, of course.'

'And nothing happened? You can tell me all about it—tomorrow over lunch,' Roy added as he saw Kane's frown.

'Foiled again. Tomorrow I'm flying home to Canada.'

Andrea felt as if icy water had been trickled down her spine. She would never see him again. Pain welled up inside her, threatening to break loose, but she clung to her role almost frantically, her face frozen, her head held so tautly that she knew she would have a headache later.

It would have been a pleasant meal if she could have relaxed, but the spectre of tomorrow was too large in her mind. What had she expected? Wasn't this dressing up to put him in his place? In any case, she was leaving tomorrow too. What had she expected him to do, take her in his arms at the last minute and tell her he would go with her, that he couldn't bear to be parted?

Rational thought didn't seem to help and all she could do was pray that she would hold her head as high to the last minute. Desperately she knew what had happened to her so suddenly: something that was only allowed in books. Love didn't happen like this. People got to know each other, became easy in each other's company. They weren't drowned by feeling so quickly. It wasn't comfortable. It hurt!

CHAPTER SEVEN

THE men were talking together and Andrea did not attempt to join in; her meal felt like sand on her tongue. Roy looked at her oddly from time to time but his attempts at flattery had died as Kane had appeared; even Roy was that bit uneasy about Kane Mallory. He was intent on scraping every last bit of information about their escape from Kane too, and Kane hardly looked at her.

'Dance with me,' Kane ordered curtly as Roy leaned back to chat with someone at the next table. It was the first time he had really looked at her since they sat down and his eyes were stormy with anger.

'Thank you, but——'

He simply stood and took her hand, pulling her to her feet, and she was in his arms before she could protest—how could she protest when they were in a crowded room? They circled the floor but she held herself stiffly away from Kane, grateful to the people who danced by and exchanged words with him, even the women.

'There's a flight to London in the morning. Will you catch that?' he asked quietly enough although she could feel anger seething inside him.

'Yes, of course. I want to see how Kip is.'

'Kip is fine. I rang this afternoon.'

'You never told me!' She looked up sharply and his gaze held hers.

'I came to tell you but you were out shopping.' His glance slid over her, lingering on the plunge of her neckline. 'Preparing your disguise.'

'I didn't bring anything suitable for dining here,' she began defensively, but he cut in harshly before she could finish.

'Nothing suitable for facing me, you mean. I take your point, Andrea. You're made of ice: cold, untouchable and perfect, like the Snow Queen.'

'This is how I am. I'm back to normal.'

'Are you?' he enquired softly, anger darkening his eyes. He pulled her abruptly to him until she was pressed against him, her legs against his, but she held herself stiffly although everything inside her began to melt.

His hand slid down her back, lingering over her satin skin, his thumb subtly tracing her spine, and she gasped, almost sagging against him.

'Now you're normal,' he muttered savagely. 'Don't play games with me, Andrea. I don't follow rules.'

It did not occur to her to deny what she had been doing; in any case, he clearly knew and the hands that held her were tight and angry as if she had been denying him something he needed, as if she belonged to him.

He held her almost cruelly for a moment and then she felt him relax, his hand sliding to her waist, teasing at the edge of her dress, and she gave up the fight as his fingers slid into the low, narrow opening and spread out over her bare skin.

'Kane!'

'Kane, people will see!' he mocked savagely. 'What do I care? This is the last time we'll dance together, my lovely, the only time. Tomorrow you fly home to Kip and Auntie and I fly out to Canada to report our losses to my father and his partner.'

'I thought *you* were Mallory?' she said shakily, trying to distract her mind from his flexing fingers.

'Oh, I am.' He smiled down at her, relenting, his teasing ended, his hand coming warmly to her back. 'My father gave up ages ago and so did Jeff Carter, but they still like to have every detail. They delight in counting losses. They're not too interested in gains now. They leave all that to me.'

'So you really are "the boss"?' Andrea said softly. 'What were you doing on a site, then?'

'From time to time, I skip the office,' he confessed with a grimace. 'I'm an engineer first and foremost and every so often the sight of glass and steel fifteen storeys high and blazoned with my name gets a bit too much for me. I flee the country and bury myself on a site and work damned hard.'

'To convince yourself that you're not rich?' Andrea surmised.

'True. Very astute, but then you are astute, aren't you? You had me spotted for a villain at once.' He looked down at her intently, his jaw suddenly tight again.

'I'm sorry,' Andrea murmured, looking away.

'Don't be.' He tilted her face and looked into her eyes, his arm tightening around her, his fingers tracing her skin. 'I'm a villain—of sorts. I have a nasty habit of taking what I want and asking later.'

She had no doubt at all about what he meant and her face flushed softly, her eyes wild.

'I want you,' he said quietly, 'but you're quite safe.'

'Because I'm Kip's sister?' Andrea asked in a choked voice.

'That and other things,' he agreed calmly. He looked down at her with cold topaz eyes and then turned her back to the table. 'Bedtime for young ladies,' he informed her sardonically. 'I'll escort you to your door and then get over to see the boys.'

No doubt he was going to sample the 'entertainment', Andrea thought miserably as she walked beside him from the lift to her door. Roy Bennet had looked surprised and grieved when they had left, but Kane had told him that Andrea was tired and would be leaving for a long flight to England next day. He really wanted to get rid of her fast. She knew that. The fact that he wanted her irritated him as if it was the first time in his powerful life that unwanted thoughts had crept into his mind. He swept everything aside that stood in his path, even if it was desire. It only assured her that his desire was distasteful to him, and the knowledge cut like a sharp knife.

He unlocked her door and handed her the key.

'Do you need any help tomorrow?' he asked coolly.

'No, thank you. I came out under my own steam—I can easily get back the same way. I'm not sixteen, after all.'

'No. You're a very clever lady. Sometimes I forget. So, goodbye, Andrea.'

It was so final, so quick she looked up at him wildly. 'Will I see you again?'

'No.' His reply was brief, utterly uncompromising, and a shiver passed over her skin at the utter finality of it, tears filling her eyes at once, shaming her. She had expected this, been prepared for it but now she was just collapsing inside.

'Don't use tears on me, Andrea,' he rasped, his face tight. 'You're not sixteen, as you pointed out. You know perfectly well what it was all about.' His lips twisted cruelly. 'I'm as much starved for a woman as the other men. You were available and very willing.'

Andrea's face went chalk-white, her dark eyes like deep pools of pain, and she slapped him hard, brushing past him and slamming her door, never stopping but walking to the bed and throwing herself down on it, sobs shaking her whole body.

Misery and humiliation swept over her. She would never see him again. She didn't *want* to! She knew as

she thought it that it was a lie. Deep down she would
grieve for Kane for a lifetime because he was not just
any man. He was too deeply in her mind to be dismissed, ever. He had rocked her whole world in such a
short time. She could still feel his arms round her.

How could he? She had been cool tonight, distancing
herself, and it had only infuriated him. He had taken
her in his arms as if she belonged to him. He had held
her close in front of everyone, not caring what they
thought, and he had reduced her to trembling so easily.
Now his cruel words had wounded her to the heart.

Her sandals fell from her feet and she buried her face
into her pillow, weeping heart-brokenly, deep, painful
sobs that shook her whole body, making her oblivious
to everything else, aware only of her own black misery.

She did not hear Kane come into her room and close
the door, his face taut as he looked at her forlorn figure.
He stood for a second watching her and then his face
twisted with some dark emotion.

He walked across, sitting beside her, and she stiffened,
knowing who it was. She would know he was there if
she was blindfolded.

'Andrea!' His hands came to her shoulders and she
twisted away wildly.

'Get out! I hate you!'

'Then you should have made sure that your door was
latched. You don't hate me, either.'

'I do!' She buried her face away from him, struggling
wildly when he reached for her. 'You think I'm just
another simpering woman, ready for some sexual
adventure.'

He jerked her up then and shook her, his face white
beneath the tan.

'Do I? If I had I would have taken you that first night,
because I wanted you the moment I saw you!'

She struggled to get away, refusing to listen, and h
pulled her to her feet, holding her arms tightly.

'You told me what it was about,' she sobbed. 'Tha
I was willing and available. I believe you, so go!'

She shook her head wildly, trying to escape, and th
pins loosened in her hair, the glittering mass of it es
caping, cascading down her shoulders.

He threaded his fingers through it, clasping her head
holding her fast, making her face him.

'If you hadn't been willing, maybe I really would hav
gone mad,' he whispered hoarsely. 'You're like a drug
I have to take in small doses because I can never los
myself in you.' His eyes moved over her face and hair
'I want you, Andrea. Every time you're near I have to
reach for you, touch you. The only way you're going to
be safe is by being thousands of miles away from m
because I burn up inside whenever you're close. I wan
to sleep with you, own you, kiss every inch of you, and
it's impossible.'

She went quite still under his hands, her face flushed
with tears, the slow stream of them still falling as sh
tried to understand what he was saying. He groaned
deeply and lifted her face to his, his tongue catching he
tears, taking them into his mouth.

'I even want to possess your tears. Do you know wha
it does to me to see you cry?' he murmured. 'All tha
gallant spirit crushed. I want to pick you up and make
love to you until you fall asleep beneath me. It's the only
thing that ever occurs to me, the only way I ever think
of for comforting you. I'm dangerous.'

He was gentle, almost humble for a minute, and her
mind sought frantically for an answer. Why had he hur
her and then come back? Why was he being so tender
now? He hadn't meant the cruel words, so why had he
said them? Why couldn't he make love to her?

'I love you.' She looked at him solemnly as she said it, her lips trembling, her mind knowing that it was quite true although she had never felt love like this before. Only the truth would do for Kane. Her eyes were still full of tears and he looked deeply into them.

'You don't,' he said quietly, his face softened. 'It's the adventure, the danger, the close proximity.'

'I'm not a fool, Kane,' she said with a catch in her voice. 'You're not the only man I've ever set eyes on.'

Suddenly his mouth was sensuous again, smiling, the golden triumph burning in his gaze.

'But I'm the only man who's ever set eyes on you. The cool Miss Forsythe who came down to dinner is the girl who faces the world. The girl who trembles in my arms is somebody you don't even know yourself. It's desire, Andrea. We both feel it and it's beautiful. Even to imagine owning you is beautiful.'

She blushed wildly, looking away, closing her eyes to escape the seduction in his, and he pulled her completely into his arms, groaning as if he was in pain.

'One minute only,' he breathed harshly. 'One minute to hold you and then I go. You'll forget all about me, Andrea.'

'I won't! I won't ever!' Tears choked her voice again and his lips slid along her cheeks, his mouth open as it met hers, his kiss heated by the same ferocity, the same necessity as she melted against him, clinging to him, sobbing his name.

They were back in the same storm of fire, locked together, but this time it was more wild because Andrea was holding nothing back, her desire as heated as Kane's, and he gasped at her response, holding her head to his, draining her sweetness desperately as if he was storing it up forever.

'Andrea!' His hands slid the dress to her waist, his fingers tightening on her slenderness before searching

for the tiny zip, and letting the black silken pool slid
to the floor.

He lifted her, placing her on the bed but this time h
came with her, his hands moving over her feverishly.

'You're so tiny aginst me, like an exquisite piece o
porcelain, silken skin, moonlit hair.'

He buried his mouth between her breasts, his hand
cupping each one, and she twisted beneath him, lost ir
a daze of passion, reaching for him as he raised himsel
to shrug out of his jacket.

His eyes burned down at her as her fingers anxiousl
tried to unfasten his shirt and he pulled off his tie
guiding her hands back to complete the task.

'Do you want to touch me, Andrea?' he murmure
huskily. 'Do you want your skin against mine? I'v
wanted that since I first saw you, so small and desirable
so angry with me.'

'I'm not angry now,' she gasped, linking her arm
around his neck, trying to pull him back to her.

He had forgotten that this was supposed to be on
minute to hold her and she prayed he would never re
member, her eyes appealing to him, beckoning until h
groaned and came down to her, the crisp dark hair or
his bronzed chest brushing her sensitive breasts and
bringing a small cry to her lips.

He looked down, his fingers caressing her, circling he
nipples as his eyes held hers, a blaze of gold that seeme
to encircle her soul. Her fingers traced his shoulders, hi
strong arms. He was like a giant, all-powerful, his hand
enclosing her and she moaned softly, her eyes pleading

'Kane!' Her desperate little murmur seemed to sna
his control and he pulled her closer, his mouth partin
hers, his tongue invading the tender moisture with roug
caresses before his teeth bit gently along her lower lip.

She gloried in his strength, in her own smallness. I
was exciting him too she knew and she twisted agains

him, raising her hips to his, feeling his thighs surge with desire. He lifted her hair, holding it to his face, kissing the length of it before taking her mouth again.

He loved her—he must! Everything about him was yearning. She entwined her legs with his, inviting him, and his hand ran down her thigh, moving inside to clasp her intimately, her name a frenzied sound in his throat. Everything turned to molten gold and Andrea threw her head back, gasping his name as his mouth covered hers almost brutally.

'I want you, Andrea! I want you so much!' His hands were lifting her, parting her thighs, his desire pushing all other thoughts to the back of his mind but her glad submission seemed to bring him to his senses and she felt the cool air against her skin as Kane rolled away, standing and gasping air into straining lungs.

It was like dying. Her hands reached out to him desperately.

'Kane! Don't leave me!'

He looked down at her, taking one of her slender hands in his, crushing it as his gaze swept over her, his mouth tight, a muscle jerking uncontrollably in his jaw.

'I've got to leave you!' The words were wrenched from his throat. 'I should never have come in. I should have left you to cry. Tomorrow you would have been out of my life and beginning to forget me.'

'No!' Her hands reached out for him but he stood like stone.

'*Yes!* I told you it was leading nowhere.'

'I love you! I don't expect anything. I'll be anything you want—your mistress——'

'I'm *married*, Andrea!' he said harshly, his eyes on her unbelieving face. 'I've been married for fourteen years!' His eyes narrowed at her distress, her face a white mask of pain. 'When you were still a schoolgirl, I was married. I still am. Forget me. An affair with you is not what I want. I've messed up your life enough as it is. Go home! When the desire has died down, you'll hate me. It's the best thing you can do!'

He bent to pick up his clothes, his discarded shirt and tie, his jacket and Andrea slowly curled up away from him, a tight curving arc of pain, her slight body too shocked for tears, too aching for remorse.

His eyes fell on the black dress and he lifted it too, looking at it for a second and then dropping it on a chair as he strode from the room. This time the latch clicked, but it wouldn't have mattered if it hadn't. He would never come back and she lay unmoving, utterly numb, waiting for the grief to hit her.

And it did. Andrea gave up any pretence of sleep. She walked about the room for the whole of the night, her arms locked around her body, cold even in her dressing-gown. Jealousy raged inside her, her mind trying to picture his wife, torturing herself with her imagination.

She tried to get her mind to be sensible, tried to tell herself that this was merely frustrated sex, but she knew it was nothing of the sort. Shamefully she knew that if Kane had wanted her she would have gone with him anyway, and that was the final blow to her self-esteem.

Morning found her pale and tired but not tired for sleep, weary deep inside, unable to believe that she would recover. She dressed carefully, making up with more attention than she had ever done in her life. She knew Kane by now. He would come for her, see her on to the aircraft whether she had told him she could manage or not. He would face it squarely and so must she.

Her silken grey trouser suit looked almost like a garment for mourning because her face was so white, startling against her fair hair. She had to stand for a few minutes and pull herself together when the knock came on the door and her eyes looked back at her as she stared into the mirror. Where was the girl who had flown out here so full of righteous indignation about her brother? Where was the girl who had walked through Oxford with swinging steps, outrageously sure of herself, satisfied about her future, her lips twitching with wry amusement as male eyes followed her progress?

The pale face that looked back at her was nobody she knew. Her eyes were smudged by shadows, her mouth trembling with tears. She opened the door resignedly and her eyes fell, not on Kane's giant stature but on the slight, apologetic form of Harry.

It was a relief, a reprieve, and she smiled at him in surprise, making herself act normally.

'Why, Harry! I'm so glad to see you. Thank you for looking after my things.'

'It was the least I could do, having to leave you and all,' he muttered, his face a little red. 'I've come to see you to your plane.'

'It's kind, Harry, but really there's no need.'

'I hope you'll let me, lass, because I don't like to disobey the boss. Kane came over to see me last night, late on. He dragged me from a good game of poker. He was off to Canada this morning but he changed his mind and left in the middle of the night. He would have taken you to the plane himself, but . . .'

'Come in, Harry,' Andrea said gently, upset by his embarrassment. Kane had not wanted to see her again and she could readily understand that. She didn't blame him, and she certainly didn't blame Harry, who now stepped into the room, his face sheepish at the sight of such unaccustomed luxury.

'I'll be ready in a minute,' Andrea said briskly, trying to put him at ease.

'There's enough time.'

'Harry, you really don't need to——'

'It's the boss's orders, Miss Andrea, and we all tend to obey Kane. If I let you talk me out of it and then anything happened I expect he'd kill me. He's a hard man, but he shoulders his responsibilities.'

Andrea winced inwardly. That's what she had become to Kane, a responsibility. Hadn't she been that since she had first seen him? Her mind tried frantically to blame her. If she had been more cool, more sophisticated... It was no use. Everywhere she looked there were Kane's golden eyes, fierce with desire. Everything ended with the one thought. Kane had reached for her hungrily, seen her and wanted her—he had said so himself. Her attempts at coldness had been savagely crushed because he had wanted to hold her and had refused to let her deny how she felt.

'I expect he wanted to get back to his wife,' she found herself saying shakily, hating herself for the words.

'I expect so.' He shot her a small glance. 'Kane's pretty close, never mentions his private life, but I expect he's got a private life, a man like him. I've known him for years and his father before him but I still don't know anything about him except how he is at work.' His face was suddenly filled with pride. 'I've been to Montreal, you know. I've seen that great big office building of his; glitters, it does. I expect he lives somewhere near by.'

Lives somewhere with his wife. Did he have any children? Was he happy? Comfortable? Her mind raced around feverishly, hurting itself, picturing his wife. He had said that he liked someone with more substance— was his wife like that? She would be well-dressed, glamorous because Kane was wealthy and his wife would have anything she needed. She would have Kane!

Andrea snapped her mind to Harry, finding him looking at her a little anxiously, and she flashed a brilliant smile at him.

'Let's go!' she said merrily, and he picked up her bag, his anxious expression relaxing. She could play this out for an hour and then she would be away, out of Africa, never to see it again as she would never see Kane. Any mourning could wait until then.

The airport was crowded and Harry moved forward like a little terrier, his wiry frame carving a path for her to the desk.

'Your plane leaves in half an hour, Miss Forsythe,' the girl told her. 'If you could go into the departure lounge?'

Andrea turned to Harry with a smile.

'I'll be fine now,' she said softly. 'Thank you, Harry, it's been nice knowing you.'

'You too, love. Remember me to Kip,' he added with a grin. 'I expect our tracks will cross again.'

'What will you do now? What will you all do?'

'We'll be back in Madembi sooner or later. Kane never gives up and eventually Okasi is going to get what's coming to him, then the dam goes on. Kane will want the old team back, Kip too.' He suddenly grinned. 'I'd have liked to see Okasi's face when Kane blew the explosives.'

'You should have seen mine!' Andrea quipped desperately. 'What will you do until then?'

'We've got leave coming and then Kane will be in touch. He keeps in contact.'

She felt like turning away at that. Kane would never be in touch with her and never was such a long time.

They shook hands and then he left and Andrea made her way to the departure lounge, sitting down to wait, her bag at her feet. Tiredness claimed her, the previous night's endless pacing catching up with her, and she bowed her head, hiding behind her fair hair. One day this ache inside would go. One day she would come back to life, be herself. People moved around her, hurrying about their business, but she didn't notice them, there was nothing she wished to see.

She looked up finally, her shoulders moving in a deep sigh, her soft mouth drooping with misery, her eyes large and dark, filling her face, staring blankly at the crowds.

Kane was there. He was standing a long way off, as far away from her as he could get. His eyes were on her though, serious and unsmiling. He was in a lightweight suit, the jacket pushed back, his hands deep into his trouser pockets.

She was frozen to the spot, unable to breathe. He was watching her, tall and unmoving, and, although he was so far away, people hurrying across her vision, there seemed to be nobody else there at all, his eyes, his face filling her world.

Her flight was called and she stood slowly, her gaze still locked with his, and he raised one hand, a final gesture as he turned away and walked out of her sight, out of her life. He hadn't left it to Harry. He had spared her the trauma, the pain of being with him but he had come to see that she was safe.

She went out to her flight, her eyes glazed with tears, but she was not sorry. Was it because he never left things to other people, because he shouldered every responsibility himself? Was it because she was Kip's sister? Or was there some spark deep down that was more than desire? She would never know. She had seen Kane for the last time and his memory would be there always, those golden eyes on her face, his tall frame coolly handsome. She would recover—one day.

Kip was still in hospital in London and she stayed there for a few days, visiting him regularly. Aunt Maureen had been frantic about her and so had Kip, but his annoyance waned at the sight of her pale face and her rather brittle form.

'You look ready to snap in two,' he said worriedly. 'I hope you didn't catch anything out there.'

'It's the heat,' she assured him quickly. 'It wasn't exactly a pleasure trip either. Getting out was very scary.'

'Thank God you were with Kane,' he said fervently, grasping her hand. 'I don't think I could trust you to anybody else. It's the last rescue operation *you'll* pull, kiddo! What did you think of Kane?' he added, a grin replacing his anxious frown. 'He's some man.'

'A furious giant,' Andrea heard herself say calmly. 'He wasn't pleased that I'd gone out to rescue you. It was a battle from the word go.'

'It was a damned silly thing to do,' he remonstrated mildly. 'I hear from television that the whole place has blown up now.'

'I saw some of it blow,' Andrea informed him, getting off the subject of Kane. It worked and she told him about her adventures, his concern mixed with admiration when she was forced to bring Kane into it.

'He'll be back,' Kip said with the utmost certainty, and Andrea nodded. She knew that. Kane never gave up. She was the only one who would never be back.

She turned the talk to her aunt and to Kip's recuperation. There was an almost feverish desire in her to hear Kane's name, but she was not some besotted schoolgirl. She knew it had to stop. She knew that she must fight out of this and struggle free. Now, though, it was too soon, the feel of his arms still too real.

She went home to see Aunt Maureen and take what was coming to her, which turned out to be tears, hugs and threats of retribution if she ever scared her aunt like that again. The cottage was too restrictive, though, too tranquil, an easy place to sit and dream impossible dreams. So Andrea went back to Oxford and her work, the discipline of learning forcing her mind to accept that life would go on, that pain would be softened eventually.

She began to pick up the old threads, accepting invitations to parties that she would normally have turned down, and an old friend and admirer became her regular companion. John Alford was a little older, almost Kip's age, and he was an easygoing companion.

'You need me, Andrea,' he assured her mockingly. 'I've been out in the world, away from the "hallowed halls". What you need is a breath of reality. You're working yourself into a breakdown. You're so thin that you're going to disappear. Work isn't the answer to everything.'

It was. It was the only way she could survive but she gave in and went out with John often, even managing to laugh and joke as weeks went by. She stored up her misery for night-time, taking it out to look at, to suffer it, like a miser with gold. Kane would not go—his image was as real now as it had been the last time she had seen him.

She kept the pain inside her for many months and then when she went home for another visit she broke down and told Kip, weeping her misery out on to his comfortable shoulder.

It was a beautiful spring day and as she parked her car and went round to the back of the cottage the smell of lilacs was almost overpowering. There was a long sweep of lawn at the back that led to the river and she smiled as she saw Kip there with a tennis ball. She had seen him slowly recover from bad injuries to his leg, worse than even Kane had thought.

There had been crutches, sticks, long hours of physiotherapy, and now he was well on the way to recovery, tossing the ball from foot to knee, keeping it in the air, making his leg work. He was a determined character in his own right and she clapped loudly at one particular manoeuvre.

He looked up and saw her for the first time, dropping the ball and moving to meet her, only a slight limp left.

'Andrea! You've developed a way of sneaking up on me. You did that the last time you were home. What's become of the "bull at a gate" sister?'

She dropped down on the garden seat beside him, smiling up at him. She had no idea what had become of the person she used to be.

'I'm sneaking up to check on your progress. How are you?'

'Better, much better, and bored to tears.' He turned to her eagerly. 'Did you read that things are back to normal in Madembi? The rebellion just folded. I had a letter from Kane yesterday—he's raring to get back to the dam.'

It was the mention of his name that did it. Andrea turned her head away quickly, catching her breath, her carefully constructed defence crumbling away.

'Hey! What is it?' Kip leaned across to try and see her face and then took her shoulders, turning her round. The tears began then and his puzzled expression changed to understanding.

'It's Kane, isn't it?' he said quietly. 'That's the reason for all this unusual quiet, this fading-away look. Oh, Andrea, love!'

He tucked her against his shoulder, his chin against her hair, rocking her as she sobbed bitterly, unable to speak.

'Didn't he want you?' he asked softly, wiping her tears as the grief spent itself.

'He's m-married, Kip!' She looked up at him with drowned eyes and he winced, pulling her back to his shoulder, his arms tightening protectively.

'Oh, lord!' he whispered against her hair.

For a long time he just held her, asking nothing, but as she subsided into small bursts of convulsive tears he looked down at her.

'Did he make love to you?'

'No. At least, not really. I'm still the same if—if that's what you mean. But it was only Kane who stopped. If he had come back, if he had wanted me, I would have… Even knowing that he was married I would still…'

Her face crumpled again and he held her tightly.

'Shh! It had to happen one day; that breezy, bossy little sister of mine had to meet a man who could make her melt. I'm sorry, love, so sorry that it had to be Kane. He's thirty-five as far as I know—I suppose it figures that he would be married.'

'He's been married for fourteen years,' Andrea whispered, her face buried against Kip's shoulder. 'He told me he was married when I was still a schoolgirl.'

He lifted her face and dried her eyes.

'If it helps at all, love, I can tell you that Kane doesn't play around. He must have really felt something.'

'He wanted me,' Andrea said quietly, 'but not enough.'

'Did you expect him to, when he was married?'

'No. I suppose that hurts as much as anything because after the first shock I know I would have… I think that knowledge made me lose all my self-esteem.'

'Not you, love, not you,' Kip assured her softly. He smoothed her hair back from her face, the old Kip who had protected her even as a boy. 'It's nearly six months. You've really got it bad, haven't you? What are you going to do?'

'Nothing.' She shrugged hopelessly. 'Work and wait for it to go away. There's nothing else to do.' She looked at him and smiled a watery smile. 'Have you ever been in love, Kip?'

'Once or twice in a half-hearted sort of way,' he joked, the smile dying away as he looked down at her. 'Nothing to make me start fading away.'

They both heard Aunt Maureen's car and Andrea jumped up in agitation, wiping at her face, but Kip urged her into the cottage.

'Nip up to your room. I'll hold her off for a minute. It's weeks since I had a bad twinge of pain. That should keep her busy until you've recovered.' He hobbled off to the kitchen, practising his act and Andrea fled up the old, oak stairs.

She had told her problems to Kip all her life and he had solved them. He couldn't solve this one but she felt easier in her mind, glad that he had faith in her, more faith than she had in herself nowadays.

CHAPTER EIGHT

IF ANYTHING it brought back the anguish, and when Andrea went back to Oxford John noticed.

'Have you been for a check-up lately, Andrea?' he asked quietly as they drove through the town on her first evening back.

'What?'

'You heard. If you get any more slender you'll collapse. It's getting worse and, don't forget, I've known you for a long time. You're not the cheeky girl I used to know.'

'It's all the hard work,' Andrea murmured defensively, but John muttered something under his breath that brought a blush to her cheeks and a gasp of shock to her lips.

'Don't give me that old tale! You're suffering. I don't know what you're suffering from but I'm worried about you.'

'Don't be,' she said quickly, her hand on his arm.

'I am.' His fingers covered hers. 'When are you going to marry me?'

'I thought you'd never ask,' Andrea joked, but he stopped the car and looked across at her seriously.

'I thought I'd never dare. I mean it.'

Andrea looked at him with shocked eyes. It had never occurred to her that John felt like that. 'You're my friend,' she reminded him softly. 'My only real friend, apart from Kip.'

'I want to be more than that, Andrea,' he said seriously. 'I know my kisses don't set you aflame. I know that some part of your clever little mind is always hidden secretly away, but it doesn't matter. I've loved you for rather a long time—for me,' he added with a sudden grin, lightening the atmosphere when he saw her stricken face.

He started the car and smiled across at her. 'Don't let it spoil your evening. I'm a very patient chap.'

She was grateful to him and she leaned across and kissed his cheek quickly. 'I can only tell you that you're the best friend I have. Where are we going, by the way?'

'I'm the best friend you have after Kip,' he corrected sternly. 'I have no illusions. As to where we're going, wait and see.'

Surprises were the joy of John's life and she hoped it wouldn't be a shock. She leaned back and smiled to herself in the darkness of the car, her smile fading when she realised that she had encouraged John's devotion because of her own loneliness. Was she now responsible for this expectation? Would she make someone else as unhappy as herself?

It was a very exclusive restaurant, well out of town, and Andrea's eyes opened wide as she went in with him. She had never thought to afford this place in all the time she had been here. She understood why he had told her to dress up well.

She went to hand over her wrap and he waited as she came out, his glance admiring on her midnight-blue dress. Her slender neck rose like the stem of a flower from the round simple neckline, the bodice hugged her breasts and tiny waist, the skirt falling into soft pleats that moved as she walked.

'John! This place costs the earth! What's the occasion?'

'Any occasion is worth it to see you looking so beautiful,' he complimented, his eyes on her softly piled up hair, looking like silver in the lights. 'However, maybe it's my birthday.'

'Oh, John! Is it? I didn't know!' She looked at him in pleading remorse as the head waiter came across to escort them and John grinned down at her.

'Never mind. It isn't, anyway.'

His arm came round her waist as she frowned at him ferociously, her lips twitching with laughter. 'You're a real devil!' she exclaimed.

'Better the devil you know,' he murmured with a leer as they looked at each other with amused affection, following a smiling head waiter, John's arm still possessively at her waist.

It wasn't until they were seated, both still laughing, that Andrea looked round. She had turned her head to smile her thanks to the waiter who solicitously held her chair and as she looked up she almost cried out with shock. A couple sat across the room, the woman beautiful, dark, her clothes speaking of wealth, her jewellery glittering in the lights. The man was tanned, handsome, cool-faced, his height apparent even when seated. His eyes met hers and held her fast. They were tawny, golden and cool as his handsome face. Kane!

Look away! Her brain sent her frantic messages that her body rejected and her eyes clung to his. Pain washed over her, pain and an excitement that she knew was madness. He was here! She could see him!

Kane inclined his head slightly, acknowledging her, his face utterly impassive and she tore her gaze away as John took her hand. She had never noticed that he had been speaking to her. She only saw Kane, she would only ever see Kane.

'Andrea? Are you all right?'

She focused her eyes on John, clinging to the reality of his presence, his affection, because now, without the hypnotic power of Kane's eyes on her, her brain caught up with her emotions. He was with a woman, a woman whose fingers glittered with rings, a golden band and a sparkling diamond. She had wondered about his wife, wept about her, and now she saw her, a statuesque brunette, flawlessly beautiful.

'Yes, of course I'm all right. I was just looking round at this fabulous place.' She did what she had been doing for months: smiled brilliantly, not removing her hand from John's warm, comforting fingers, her defence mechanism perfected over the weary months of never seeing Kane.

'You looked as if you'd seen a ghost.'

'It's the fear of the bill. I refuse to wash up,' she joked, laughing into his eyes, and he was fooled, as everyone but Kip was fooled.

Oh, please, let me hold myself together, she prayed silently. Don't let me break up in front of him. I want him to know that I was just as he said: filled with the excitement of the adventure, the danger. She poured her attention on John and he squeezed her hand, his eyes making her feel the dread of guilt, but she couldn't draw back now, not until Kane had left.

They were into their main course when she sensed movement at Kane's table and a glance from beneath her thick lashes told her he was leaving. He helped the woman to her feet and they exchanged some joke, her hand coming to his arm as her head tilted back. It was her left hand and Andrea closed her eyes. She didn't want to see those rings again. Why was he here? Did fate have to bring him to this place on this night? Did she have to see the woman he had loved for more than ten years and forgotten only briefly in a blaze of passion?

She forced herself to eat, to look only at John, to listen intently when he spoke, and when she looked round they had gone. It was like the end of all light, the beginning of a long silence, because one look at Kane had told her that the misery would never end. It would never grow less either. Just once in a lifetime a man came along who was the master of her soul and he belonged to someone else.

She was silent on the return trip, glad of the darkness, moving the side mirror stealthily when the headlights of a following car threatened to show her white face to John's worried eyes. He was still worried when he pulled up, outside her flat.

'Let me come in with you,' he begged softly, his arm sliding round her when she started to move. 'I don't know what it is, but whatever is wrong with you it's worse now.'

'I'm all right, John,' she assured him but she couldn't force a smile. Her face was tight with pain.

He took her in his arms frustratedly, his lips covering hers, his hand cupping her cold face. She did not struggle. If he wanted to kiss her he could, because nothing could reach her. He drew her more tightly to him, feeling her lack of response, trying to force feelings on her that just were not there, but she was cold in his arms.

The headlights of a car swung across them, bathing them in brilliance for a second and John swore softly under his breath as she jerked away, a strange feeling in her that she was betraying all she felt for Kane. There was the feeling that he knew somehow that it mattered, it mattered terribly. The darkness after the brilliant light was a refuge and John did not attempt to kiss her again.

'I'll ring in an hour to see that you're all right,' he said quietly.

'Don't bother, John,' she begged, reaching up to kiss him affectionately on his cheek. 'I'll be asleep.'

'Do you ever sleep, Andrea?' he asked with soft bitterness, and she did not answer. She could understand his bitterness and she had to stop seeing him. One broken heart was all she could take. She didn't want John's on her conscience.

The next day she abandoned everything and went home. She couldn't risk seeing Kane again. She had no idea why he was in Oxford. For one moment she had thought he had brought his wife there deliberately, but the thought was squashed as it was born. He wouldn't do that. He would know there was a chance that they would meet and he would never even think of such a thing. Why he was here was not really the issue. She had to leave if he was here and, in any case, she needed Kip.

There was no refuge. As soon as Kip saw her face, he knew.

'You've seen Kane,' he said flatly, and she could only nod in misery.

'He phoned me,' Kip said. 'He's gathering the old team to go back out to the dam and he wanted to know how I was.'

She just looked at him and he added, 'He asked about you. I know it's no help at all, but he did.'

'What did he say?' she asked wearily, sinking to a chair, throwing her bag and coat to another.

'Just a polite enquiry. "And how is Andrea?" Nothing more. Typical Kane.'

'He was in Oxford,' she said dully. 'His wife was with him.'

Kip's face reddened with instant rage and she wished she had held her tongue.

'That was bloody cruel!' he snapped, but she shook her head, her fair hair falling softly around her face.

'No. It was sheer chance. He wouldn't be cruel to me.'

'Maybe you don't know him as well as I do, Andrea. I've seen Kane as cold as ice, utterly untouchable.'

'So have I,' she assured him quietly. 'I've also seen him caring, thoughtful and gentle.'

'Nothing will ever change your mind, will it?' Kip asked despondently, and she smiled, shaking her head.

'I survived. I was with John and he's a good cover. I then ran for home, to my lair and you.'

He came and sat on the arm of her chair, his hand stroking her hair.

'What about John? He could get serious. Is it fair?'

'No. It's not fair and he is getting serious. I can't see him much more. I already have enough on my conscience with how I feel about Kane.'

He tilted her face and met her eyes. 'You did nothing wrong. It never happened. Nobody betrayed his wife, neither of you.'

Her mind slid treacherously to Kane, to his lips on hers, to his fierce possessive kisses, his raging desire. If she had been his wife, she would have felt betrayed.

'You're my knight in shining armour still,' she said, smiling up at Kip.

'Except that I can't slay the dragon,' he pointed out ruefully. 'You're in love with him.'

Hiding away in Derbyshire was not possible. Andrea knew that distance meant nothing at all as far as her feelings were concerned and she could not go on keeping out of Kane's way. She had no idea why he had been in Oxford and in all probability he would already have left. She returned, much of her journey spent in trying to come up with a way of breaking it easily to John. If they could just have remained friends she would have been happy at that but it was not going to be enough for John and sadly she knew that her friendship with him had to end, for his own sake.

She contacted him the next day, disgusted with herself to feel a surge of relief when he was too busy to meet her. It was short-lived.

'We'll have afternoon tea in town,' he suggested eagerly. 'I can scrounge off for about half an hour. I'll meet you there.'

He rang off before she could protest and she knew it would be just another time of putting things off. She could hardly tell John the sorry news in the middle of a tea-shop with people around them. She could imagine how he was going to take it and she had to spare him any embarrassment.

At three-thirty she was waiting outside, pacing back and forth, and John appeared almost instantly, his beaming smile bringing an answering smile to her lips.

'You phoned me as soon as you got back,' he reminded her happily, kissing her cheek. 'Things are looking up.' He tucked her hand under his arm and led her inside. 'I've missed you badly. Don't go skipping off again.'

Andrea smiled but it was an effort. She couldn't let this go on. The way John held her arm close to his, the way he took such care of her all told its own story. Guilt came flooding back. She had to tell him now.

The café was in an old wine cellar, a place beloved by tourists and students alike, and it was fairly full at the moment, people they knew either nodding to them or calling out as they passed.

'John, Andrea! Sit over here with us.'

Two of the men from college called to them but John grinned and shook his head. 'Forget it. I'm not sharing her with you two. I've only just got her back.'

He urged her on to the accompaniment of soft boos and hisses, everybody laughing. Andrea was laughing too but her laughter was uneasy. How was she going to tell John?

He leaned over her, his arm coming round her shoulders and when she looked up he grinned widely.

'No cause for violent alarm,' he whispered against her ear. 'I'm just staking a very obvious claim. Both of those chaps have got their eye on you.'

'John. I've got to talk to you,' she began desperately, but he merely handed her into a seat.

'Over tea and scones.' He suddenly looked up and muttered under his breath. 'Hell! There's Prof Reeves. I was going to skip his lecture and take you on from here for a drive and then dinner. If he sees me he'll start talking and I'll have to leave with him.'

'Where?' Andrea's face flushed as she realised that she was grasping at the chance to put off the time to tell John.

'Table by the window. Big chap with him, very big chap,' John mused.

Andrea looked round then, her eyes searching for Professor Reeves, all the colour fading from her face as she saw Kane sitting beside him. He was still here! Haunting her! She just stared at him hopelessly and his eyes met hers but this time he did not incline his head politely. This time he smiled, a slow, twisted smile that contained an edge of cruelty.

She looked away quickly, glad to find that John had been busy with their order and had not seen her expression. She dared not raise her eyes again. Kane here and looking at her like that. There had been nothing in his expression to denote kindness. She knew that cruel smile, those narrowed eyes.

'You wanted to talk to me.' John leaned across to her, reminding her why she had rung him in the first place, but she shook her head, giving him a shaken smile.

'Not now, John. Not here. I—I'll tell you later.'

'It's not that you're ill?' he asked with sudden anxiety, and she put her hand over his quickly, smiling up at him.

'No. Stop worrying about me. It's nothing like that at all. I can't talk to you here.' She could still feel Kane's eyes coldly on her and it had robbed her of any confidence.

'Looks as if chance would be a fine thing,' John muttered. 'The prof just looked up and saw me. Brace yourself.'

Professor Reeves bore down on their table with a good deal of speed considering his age and weight. He was intent on capturing John and started talking even before he had reached them.

'There you are, my boy! Stroke of luck. I've been looking at that experiment and it seems to me to have exciting possibilities. Come over and join me. We'll talk.'

He had John's arm in a tight grip and John just had time to drop money on the table and snatch up Andrea's hand as he was almost dragged away. It did catch the professor's attention though and he included her in his beaming smile.

'Of course you must come too, my dear. Rude of me not to have spoken. How's your aunt?'

'Er—very well, thank you,' Andrea muttered, terrified now that she had to face Kane close up.

He rose smoothly to his feet, an enigmatic smile on his lips.

'Andrea.' He nodded at her politely now but his eyes were filled with irony, glittering and cold, and John glanced at her face and then looked sharply across at Kane, realisation dawning slowly but very surely. He was captured now by the professor but he seemed to be listening very little; his eyes were on Andrea's pale face and her heart sank at the forlorn look about him. Was she that obvious? Did Kane see it too?

Why was he here? Had Kip been right after all? Was this some perverse whim of cruelty because he had desired her and now resented it? She looked up at him to find his eyes coldly on her face and she couldn't look again.

'By Jove! I've got a lecture!' Professor Reeves stood and looked around a little wildly. 'Almost forgot. Come along, my boy.' He dragged an angry and reluctant John to his feet and then glanced across at Andrea and Kane. 'Most remiss,' he muttered. 'Kane, can you take care of...?'

'Andrea!' John snapped, almost jerking his arm away. 'I can take care of her myself.'

'It's all right, John,' she managed quietly, her face flooded with colour. 'I can walk home by myself. It's only two streets away.'

'Are you sure, love?' He was inclined to be aggressive, something she had never seen in John, and Andrea nodded quickly.

'I'm quite sure. I'll go now.'

He allowed himself to be marched out, the professor talking energetically, but he glanced back at the door and looked relieved to see her gathering her bag and preparing to leave.

Kane had sauntered over to the other table and to her astonishment came back with her tea and the plate of scones.

'You never got to your light refreshments,' he said sardonically, putting them in front of her.

'I don't want any.' She got up to leave, but this was Kane, not John.

'Of course you do.' His hand came to her shoulder, powerful as ever, his grip tightening when she looked as if she was about to walk off. 'Sit down. You wouldn't have been here if you hadn't wanted tea.'

'I merely wanted to talk to John,' she muttered, avoiding his eyes.

'Hard luck. You were outclassed there. The prof can talk more than anyone I know.' He glanced at her in amusement when she took a gulp of tea and mutinously crushed a scone under her fingers. 'Does he know your aunt?'

'No. He doesn't even know me.'

'That's brain power run riot. Take note,' Kane murmured mockingly. 'He constantly asks after my grandfather, whom he never even met and who has been dead these twenty years. He can just about keep my identity in his mind, providing that experiments don't intrude.'

'How do you know him?' Andrea took her courage firmly in hand and met his taunting gaze. If he could talk so coolly, then so could she.

'He's my godfather. I'm staying with him. A duty when I'm in England. I take messages back and forth from my father and old Carter to the prof. I've just been driving him into town for his lecture but he can't forgo the tea and scones here.'

'Why are you in England?' Andrea asked, fighting down misery and allowing hostility to surface at the cool mockery in his eyes. He was acting as if nothing at all had happened between them.

'I'm on business. I have to see contacts in London and this is the best place to be. I get enough of the big city living in Canada. Oxford's a very nice place to stay, but I suppose you know that?'

'I'm here to work. I prefer to be at home in Derbyshire,' Andrea said stiffly, looking away again and crumbling her scone even more.

'But you don't work all the time. I saw you out to dinner the other night and here you are now.' How could he bring that up, when he had been with his wife? Was he just cruelly reminding her? The memory of lying in his arms intruded and she felt a wave of bitterness.

'I'm allowed time off for good behaviour,' she snapped waspishly and he was highly amused at his own ability to goad her, apparently. At any rate, he laughed and she stood with a very decisive movement, gathering her bag again.

'I have to go now. Goodbye.'

'I'll take you home.' He stood too and nodded to the waitress, leaving the money on the table and accompanying her to the door.

'There's no need whatever. I can walk the couple of streets to my flat with no difficulty. I've been walking since I was twelve months old.'

She set off but he was beside her in one stride, his hand like steel on her arm.

'I'll take you. I want to know where you live in any case, then I can pick you up for dinner tonight.'

His cool cheek stunned her. Was he going to bring his wife or leave her behind? She turned furious eyes on him. 'No, thank you. I have a date for dinner. You just saw the professor drag him reluctantly away.'

'I saw you pacing restlessly outside, waiting for him. The boyfriend?' he enquired with a tight smile.

'The very same,' Andrea snapped. What did he mean by coming here and inviting her to dinner? He might be staying with Professor Reeves for a very good reason but his wife was with him. She had seen her with her own eyes. In any case, she was not about to sink under the swell of the tide again. Kane was taunting, mocking, goading, and he was not the man she remembered at all. He was more like the man she had first seen in Africa. Maybe this was the way to get him out of her bloodstream, to have him here so that she could recall her first feelings.

'He's serious, I take it?' Kane asked quietly, looking straight ahead as she walked reluctantly beside him.

'Very serious. He asked me to marry him.'

'And of course you said yes?'

'Not yet. We both have a lot to do. I have my doctorate and John is here to do some research; he's a biochemist.'

'A combination of brain power,' he drawled sarcastically. 'Your children should be interesting.'

'Are yours?' Andrea asked bitterly.

'I don't have any,' he murmured. 'The question never arose.'

Suddenly her anger vanished and she felt only hurt. There was a tight restraint about Kane that communicated itself to her and she wanted to get away fast. Being close to him was doing terrible things to her. It even hurt that he had been watching her as she waited outside the tea-shop. He had been looking at her and she hadn't even known. She felt as if a few precious minutes had been lost to her.

'I can manage by myself, thank you. I only live up here.'

'I may as well walk the rest of the way. It's a nice afternoon.'

Short of running wildly off there was nothing she could do about it, and her eyes scanned the streets hopefully for somebody she knew, somebody who would give her a good excuse to bid him a calm goodbye and walk off. There wasn't a friendly face in sight. She had heard it said that when you wanted a policeman there wasn't one to be seen; neither was there a friend or even an acquaintance. She walked on in silence and Kane strode beside her impassively.

'I live here.' She stopped at the big old house where she had her flat and Kane looked up at the height of it.

'Old and impressive.'

'It is. Unfortunately it's not mine. I only have the bottom flat. I couldn't even manage that without help.'

'The boyfriend,' he concluded drily, glancing down at her with unwarranted contempt.

'The brother!' she snapped, her voice choking. 'Kip pays my rent and also bought my car. If you want to know anything else, write to me!'

She snatched her keys from her bag and strode off up the steps and she didn't look back. It was only when she got inside, the door firmly closed behind her, that she let the tension drain from her. Her legs were shaking. They had been shaking since she had seen Kane in the café, and she walked through to her small sitting-room and sank to the settee.

Wild thoughts of running back to Kip came into her head but she refused to let them stay there. Kane was here with his wife. She had never been in any doubt about that. So what was so very different?

She knew without much thought. Kane was different. He had been icily cold, his humour sheer habit, his impatience barely concealed. Walking back had been a polite gesture, just like the invitation to dinner. Any desire he had had for her was gone and she was forced back to the conclusion he had pointed out so many months ago. It had been the danger, close proximity, the spice to an adventure. It was all more dead than before. She could no longer dream that he wanted her but was not free. Now there was not even that.

She put off telling John. The experiment seemed to be occupying most of his time and for a few days they saw each other rarely. She wanted a quiet time to tell him gently and the occasion just didn't arise. She saw nothing of Kane. At first she almost crept about when she was in town, ready to run at the first sight of him, but he never appeared and she concluded that he had finally left. It should have filled her with relief but it only made each day blank and painful.

The time for the Commem. Ball came and she resolutely decided that this was the place to tell John. Their weekends of going about together were now a thing of the past. Both of them were snowed under with work and the inevitable could not be put off any longer. When he called for her she would tell him.

The Commem. Ball was a big occasion and she dressed with care. It was a chance for all the women to wear some long and glamorous dress and Andrea wore her favourite. It was not new but she had never worn it here before and she was well aware of how it looked. She rarely wore white. Her hair was so pale that she was convinced that in white she would look colourless, but this was a dress her aunt had bought for her the previous year and with it on she revised her opinion.

She swirled round in front of the mirror and clouds of dreamy chiffon moved around her, settling back like softly falling snow as she stopped. The bodice was smoothly fitting to her breasts, the neckline gathered low and caught with glittering stones, leaving her shoulders bare. She had set her hair high, softening it around her face, and she deliberately kept her make-up to the minimum, a pale lip gloss and dark eye-shadow to deepen her eyes.

John stopped in the doorway when he called for her and took one deep, seething breath.

'You look—astonishing,' he muttered, his eyes running over her. He met her gaze ruefully. 'How you look to-night tells me something I should have guessed a long time ago. I've been worried about your brittle looks, your unhappy eyes, and I've been imagining you were ill and not telling me. I must be some sort of idiot.' He leaned in the doorway and looked at her levelly. 'It's a man, isn't it?'

Andrea looked at him sadly.

'I was going to tell you tonight. I—I've put off telling you because...'

'Because you didn't want to hurt me,' he finished astutely. 'It was that trip to Africa, wasn't it? Old Reeves was babbling on at me about Kane Mallory. It's him.'

'Yes. I'm sorry, John.' She looked down at her clenched hands and he walked into the room, closing the door quietly.

'He looked as if he would have liked to kill you. What happened? Did you turn him down too?'

Andrea winced at the soft bitterness in his voice. 'He's married.'

For a minute John said nothing and then he moved forward and pulled her gently into his arms, his hand holding hers.

'My poor love.' He said nothing else, just went on holding her, and Andrea fought off tears, tears for both of them.

'I'm so sorry, John,' she choked. 'I should have told you sooner. I had no idea that you felt—felt so... I suppose I clung to you as I cling to Kip. Both of you make me happy, as happy as I can be under the circumstances, and selfishly I didn't want it to end.'

'And who says it's going to end?' he enquired drily, tilting her face and smiling down at her with an arrogance that was quite new. His sudden grin took the edge off it and he gave her a hug. 'You've just paid me a very great compliment. You've told me that I make you happy and you've put me in the same category as the mighty Kip. If you think you're sending me away for my own good then you can think again. Anyway, I might never marry. Sometimes I rather fancy being like Prof Reeves. He's a crafty old coot.'

Andrea looked up into his eyes and smiled through tears.

'Oh, John. You're so...'

'Wonderful,' he supplied. 'Wonderful is the word you seek. Now dry your tears and let's go. I'm going to spend all evening basking in your glamour.' He went to open the door as she picked up her bag and when she looked up he was smiling at her ruefully, a great deal of affection on his face.

'Come on, good buddy,' he said quietly. 'I'm quite prepared to stand back for any man you love, but if anyone else looks closely at you tonight I'll flatten them.'

It was a heavy weight lifted from her heart and mind and Andrea sat beside him on the way and made a steady count of her blessings. She had a happy home, a good future, a brother who adored her and a friend who put her feelings before his own. She had so much more than many people had. If she could only stop thinking about Kane, stop remembering...

As usual the organisers had done them proud. It was a glittering occasion with everyone there, the atmosphere so sparkling that Andrea relaxed and allowed herself to be simply swept along on the sheer magic of the event. It was almost like Christmas. Balloons and streamers hung from the old vaulted ceiling of the college hall, there was a good professional band and the food was superb, a huge buffet set down one side of the great hall, the tables draped with ribbons and flowers.

John had never been so gentle and they were constantly at the centre of groups of laughing people. Students and professors mingled, invited guests from the town joined in and Andrea realised with a little shock that she was enjoying herself. It brought a sparkle to her eyes and John looked down at her as they danced and smiled knowingly.

'What did I tell you?' he murmured. 'An occasion like this every night and you'll be right as rain in no time. I'll have to see what I can arrange.' He swirled her round to the music and they were both smiling when she felt his arm tighten. The movement was almost imperceptible but it brought instant tension to Andrea.

'He's here, isn't he?' she whispered and John held her closely.

'Yes. He's just walked in with the prof. There's a woman with him.'

She just nodded. There would be. He could hardly leave his wife at home if he had been invited to the ball here. She just prayed he would ignore her, that she could rely on John to keep her clear.

CHAPTER NINE

JOHN had every intenton of protecting Andrea but they had both reckoned without the professor. He collared them as they went to the buffet.

'It's working, my boy!' He pounced on John and met a blank stare.

'I see no evidence of it,' John muttered grimly, his eyes openly hostile as Kane and his wife moved with the professor and joined them. His hand tightened on Andrea's as he felt her tremble. 'We'll talk about it tomorrow, Professor Reeves,' he added firmly when his obscure remark brought a look of terror to the old man's face. 'Tonight, we're enjoying ourselves.'

'Of course.' The professor looked as if he would have liked to introduce Kane but was apparently dumbfounded that he couldn't remember his name. The woman's eyes twinkled with instant understanding but Kane didn't even notice. He was looking at Andrea with a cold bitterness that shook her to the core. Did he imagine she was going to blurt out everything to his wife? She went even paler and was almost shaking visibly when John nodded curtly to everyone and swept her away.

He swore under his breath.

'Why the hell can't he get back to where he came from and take her with him?' he rasped quietly.

'He's staying with Professor Reeves. The professor is his godfather. I think he's an old friend of the family.'

'At this moment I could boil the prof in olive oil!' John snapped. 'As to Mallory, maybe this will show you what he really is. He must have known you'd be here tonight. Face it, love, he doesn't care at all that this is hurting you.'

No, he didn't care. Andrea knew that with utmost certainty. For some cruel reason he seemed to be almost haunting her. He knew what it did to her to see his wife there. Every part of her seemed to be filled with pain. The more she saw Kane, the more she loved him. Being apart had not eased things; her feelings had only grown.

'Do you want to leave?' John asked more gently, looking down at her pale face.

'No. I was enjoying it. I'm going to go on doing that. They're not driving me out.'

'Attagirl!' John whispered, but he didn't sound too convinced and as Andrea danced on decidedly shaky legs she wasn't too convinced either. There was just this burning need to be close to Kane, in his arms. If he would only smile at her it would be something to remember but he was doing no such thing. There had been a bitter resentment in his eyes as if she were all to blame. It was easy to believe that now he hated her.

She resolutely concentrated on John and the many friends they had. Every time her eyes started to search for Kane she controlled them firmly. She had the unhappy feeling that he was watching her coldly and it made her force herself into a nervous brilliance that everyone mistook for happiness. She was so glowing, so glamorous that she coud have danced with almost any man there if John had allowed it.

'If you're going to collapse in a heap then I'm going to be there to catch you,' he muttered as he side-tracked yet another would-be partner. 'Keep this up and I'll be taking you to hospital on the way back.'

'I'm all right,' she assured him, her smile brilliant.

'Are you?' he muttered angrily. 'You're dying on your feet. I could kill him!'

'It's all sheer chance,' she whispered shakily. 'It—it just happened that——'

John swore bitterly under his breath. 'Stop making excuses for him! He's doing it on purpose. We both know that. He's a bastard, and the sooner you allow yourself to see that the better!'

Perhaps. But she loved him, she loved him as fiercely as he had held her, as overpoweringly as he had kissed her. His name was ringing round in her mind like a mournful bell.

It was the woman who finally brought things to a head, and that quite innocently. They were back at the buffet when she came up with Kane and, as Andrea glanced up and as quickly looked away, she found herself unable to escape.

'Nobody is about to introduce me so I'm going to introduce myself,' she announced with a smile at Andrea. 'I'm Adele, and I know for sure that you must be Andrea.'

Andrea's heart almost stopped and John looked as if he was about to take a chance and hit Kane there and then. Kane saved him the trauma of it.

'Harry was singing your praises to Adele,' he explained stonily, his glance narrowed on the pallor of Andrea's face. 'He also gave a glowing description.'

'Not glowing enough,' Adele murmured, her eyes sweeping over Andrea's pale beauty. 'I can hardly imagine you fighting your way through jungle.'

'She's tougher than she looks,' Kane bit out with very little subtlety.

'Not a very nice thing to say,' Adele remonstrated softly, glancing at him in surprise. 'You'd better dance with her and tell her you're not quite the brute you seem to be.'

They all stood quite stunned but she had no idea apparently that she had blundered so gently into a turmoil of anger and dismay. She turned to John, who stood unbelieving.

'Can you reach that piece of pie for me? It's a bit too far away for me to get and I've been eyeing it greedily for ages.'

It was astonishing how innocence could defeat the most carefully laid plans. John turned away to obey, his face almost dazed, and Andrea felt Kane's hard hands on her as he led her back to the dance-floor.

'I—I don't want——' she began anxiously but Kane's fingers almost bruised her.

'I can well believe it,' he assured her stonily. 'However, Adele expects it and a scene right here is not really your style. We fight in private, if you recall.'

'I don't recall anything,' Andrea whispered shakily, but he swung her into his arms, looking over her head as if she weren't there.

'That's not strictly true. You remembered to get yourself a man who could take your hand and tell you when it was bedtime.'

'Some advice is too good to ignore,' she said bitterly. 'I took it to heart.'

His hands tightened painfully.

'Very speedily,' he observed tightly.

It was all hurting so much. In spite of her determination to keep as cold as Kane she felt everything begin to break up inside. His grip was cruel and he was only holding her because his wife had been astonished at his rude remark.

'Your wife is very nice,' Andrea said quickly, desperate to bring the conversation on a different tack. It did no good. Kane glanced down at her icily.

'You have second sight? That really surprises me.'

'I—I don't need second sight to make my mind up about somebody. She looks gentle.'

He drew back to look at her and found her eyes gazing wistfully at the woman with John.

'Adele is my sister,' he grated impatiently. 'Don't worry about her stealing your true love. She's happily married.'

Andrea didn't know what to say. For a moment she felt only happiness that he hadn't brought his wife here where he knew she would see them both. It hadn't been a cruel trick. The relief made her tremble.

'I—I thought she was your wife. I thought——'

'What did you think?' he rasped. 'Adele loves England. Every chance she gets to come with me, she does. Her husband works away for a lot of the time as I do and I suppose she could get lonely but she's a born survivor. She was stuck with the prof as a godfather too.'

'I—I'm sorry. I didn't mean... When you said you were married I——'

'When I said I was married, I meant it,' he bit out callously. 'If I hadn't been married you would now have the problem of explaining to your intended why you were not a sweet little virgin! I wish to God I'd taken you!'

She tried to pull away, shocked to her heart, but he just tightened her closer, his hand biting into her waist.

'Let me go.' The words just burst out through trembling lips, a sob at the back of her voice, and he drew back a little, looking down at her. She tried to face him with anger but her face looked almost drawn, her lips trembled, and in spite of her fight for control tears glazed her dark eyes, hung on her long lashes.

Pain seemed to flash across his tanned face and for a moment his hand lifted towards her tears but it dropped away, his tawny eyes blazing down at her.

'Damn you, Andrea,' he said in that soft menacing voice she remembered so well, bitterness adding to the threat. 'I wish I'd never set eyes on you.'

They just stared at each other, making no pretence of dancing, Kane's eyes almost on fire with anger, and John came up like an avenging angel.

'Let her go!' John's voice was choked with rage and Kane just turned away, his hands falling to his sides.

'With pleasure,' he rasped. 'She's all yours.'

John pulled her into his arms, dancing her away, trying to retrieve something of the situation and giving her time to calm down, but she knew she would not do any such thing and so did he. The hurt was now too deep for recovery.

'Take me home, John,' she pleaded quietly. 'Please take me home.'

Long after John had gone, Andrea sat staring at the wall. She had had a shower and changed to her dressing-gown and she cuddled into it for comfort, but the thought of sleep was far from her mind. The evening had left her feeling shocked and weak, utterly hopeless. That Kane had not brought his wife made no difference at all except that he had not been practising that particular cruelty. He had been cruel in many other ways, though, and she could still hear his harsh voice, his caustic reminder of how she had been in his arms.

He had sounded bitter, as if in some way she had betrayed him. Did he expect her to spend the rest of her life mourning for him? What did he care if she really *had* been going to marry John? Kane was already married; his life had been settled for fourteen whole years and now he wished he had taken advantage of her love for him and *then* told her about his wife.

It was a thought that would never leave her head. It assured her that any lingering thoughts she had had of Kane loving her deep down were stupid. He had simply wanted her and now he wished he had taken her. Things were exactly as they had been when he had left her that night at her door in Nairobi. She had been available and willing.

Why had fate been so vicious in making her meet him again? All her carefully built barriers would have to be rebuilt and sometimes she thought a whole lifetime would not be enough. She had never hurt as she was hurting now.

She was worn out with weeping, but when she eventually went to bed she simply tossed about until finally she got up and took two aspirin. She had developed a searing headache to add to her troubles and it looked as if the night was about to go on forever. In the end, exhaustion won and she fell into a deep sleep.

The sound of the doorbell woke her after a long time and before she could even get out of bed somebody was also hammering on the door. If she hadn't been so bemused by lack of sleep and aspirin she would have been alarmed, but all she could think of was that it was almost two o'clock, with everyone else in the town probably asleep.

It was only as she struggled into her dressing-gown, almost deafened by the constant pounding on the door and the sound of the bell that kept pace with it, that she began to feel uneasy. There was nobody in the house but herself. The other two tenants had moved out last week, their leases not to be renewed, and she had the whole place to herself for the moment. She crept to the door, not that anyone outside would hear her over the din they were creating.

'Who is it?' she managed quite firmly in a small interlude of silence.

'Open the door, Andrea!'

Kane's voice was almost unrecognisable and she gasped with shock, trembling at once. 'Go away! I—I won't let you in! Whatever you want it will keep until tomorrow.'

'You'll let me in or I'll break the door off its hinges.'

He wasn't shouting. His voice was low and threatening, and when she didn't immediately answer he began hammering on the door again. If he went on like that the police would soon be summoned by some good citizen and Andrea could imagine the embarrassment of that. She also knew his powerful physique. Breaking the door off the hinges was in no way beyond him. She unlocked the door and found Kane glaring down at her.

'What do you want?'

He looked utterly wild and she stepped back with a small burst of fear. She had seen him angry but never quite like this. His jacket was slung over his shoulder, his tie pulled loose, his hair untidy. The man who had danced with her, taunted and insulted her at the ball had quite disappeared. He was still in evening dress, but he looked as if he had been walking about for hours.

He just walked in and looked round closely, then he flung his jacket down as Andrea watched him in a daze.

'You—you can't come in here, Kane,' she began with as much spirit as she could muster. 'If you've been drinking——'

'I thought about it.' He looked down at her with so much fury that she moved involuntarily behind the settee. 'I decided against it, though. It dulls the senses and I need all mine tonight. I'm not here for a chat.'

'Please go, Kane,' she whispered, her hand shaking as she pushed the fair hair back from her forehead. 'I—I'm tired. I've only just got to bed.'

'And all by yourself. Didn't you feel up to it tonight?' he snarled. 'I know he's gone or he'd be out here now, ready to fight for you. Plenty of men looked ready to fight for you tonight, Andrea. You looked like a beautiful little ghost in the white dress. I remember you wore a black one for me. Was that significant?'

She was suddenly frightened of his rage, frightened of his power. The white silk shirt did nothing to disguise his superb strength and he seemed to be hating her.

'Please, Kane——' she began but he cut in ruthlessly.

'I've heard that before, but you weren't begging me to leave. You were begging me to stay. I heard other words too, words that said, "I love you". Do you say that to him?'

He looked bitter, haggard, and she swayed, putting her hand out to the settee, sure she would faint.

Her action brought a changed expression to his face, the sneer fading from his eyes, leaving them alert and impossibly golden.

'What's the matter with you?' He rounded the settee, grasping her arms before she could escape. 'What are you taking? My God! Is that why you look so pale, so thin? What are you taking?'

'Nothing, Kane!' She tried to pull away but his hands were like steel, digging into her, and when she struggled he shook her hard.

'Answer me!'

'I—I had a headache. I took two aspirin.'

'Aspirin wouldn't make you look like this. Do you think I'm blind?'

'I'm tired. I—I've been sleeping badly. It's an accumulation——'

'Of late nights, overwork and sex?' he rasped, shaking her again. 'It must be some relationship. I've seen you when you were exhausted. You never looked as if you were dying!'

'What I do with my life is none of your business,' Andrea managed in a stifled voice, his insults finally bringing some life to her. 'The adventure we shared does not give you the right to pursue me and demand explanations of my conduct. The adventure ended a long time ago. I'm just—just someone you met once.'

'We did more than meet,' he reminded her in a curiously husky voice. 'Much more.'

Colour flooded her pale skin, memory bringing a tremble to her lips.

'I'm marrying John,' she lied, her only defence against this attack. 'I stepped back into my old life with no difficulty whatever. John was waiting for me. Until you suddenly appeared in Oxford, I'd forgotten all about you.'

He let her go at once but did not move away and when she looked up at him those same amber eyes were blazing down at her, holding her gaze in spite of her efforts to break the contact. He took her face between two strong hands, hurting and then cradling it between his fingers.

'I'll go,' he said more quietly. 'I've never behaved like a fool in my life and it's too late to start now. Do you know why I came here tonight? I came here because I want you. I can't stop wanting you. It's an ache in my gut that refuses to go away. I know what I can do to you, how I can change that cool little poise you have. Tonight you were going to be mine because wanting you is eating away at me and soon you'll belong to somebody else.'

There was so much raw feeling in his eyes that she opened her mouth to tell him it wasn't true, but nothing was changed—she remembered that in time and it saved her. He was married, even though desire still ate at him as it did at her.

She would never have had the chance to tell him, though. Something in her changed expression weakened his self-control and he caught her up, lifting her off her feet, crushing her in his arms as his lips covered hers in a searching, painful kiss.

'Andrea! Andrea! I've got to talk to you,' he groaned against her mouth. 'You've got to listen to me. But first I've got to hold you, kiss you. I've got to touch you again. I need to!'

His lips came back to hers, possessive, demanding, the Kane she remembered, claiming her as if he knew he had the right. And she couldn't breathe, couldn't move. The scent of his skin seemed to surround her, the fierce masculine body bringing an instant reaction inside her.

She felt her arms lifting to cling to him, her body softening to accept his demands, and panic overwhelmed her, Kip's words rising to the top of her mind, reminding her that she had not helped to betray Kane's wife. If she let herself drown in Kane's arms as her whole being wanted to she would betray his wife now—and herself too. He belonged to another woman, a woman he had left behind, a woman who suspected nothing.

She pulled her face away, twisting her head, controlling her voice with an effort she hadn't realised she was capable of.

'Let me go, Kane. I don't know you. I don't want to. I've known John for years and I'm going to marry him very soon.'

It came out coldly, bitterly, and he took her trembling to be disgust. He also looked disgusted with himself as he lowered her to her feet.

'All right, my little virgin. I'll not spoil your wedding-day,' he promised hoarsely.

'How do you know that——?' she began bitterly but his hand tilted her chin, his fingers uncompromising and steady although his breath was still an uneven sound in his throat.

'I know you, Andrea, silky little Andrea,' he taunted pitilessly. 'It's all or nothing with you. I thought the ''all'' was for me but I can see I was wrong. Your condition is obviously the result of overwork because your lips still taste the same. If I didn't know better I would believe they had been waiting for me, as if I'd only just left them for a minute.' He stared down at her as if he'd never seen her before. 'You melt when I touch you and you're going to marry somebody who hasn't the faintest idea of how you react to me. I pity the poor devil!'

She hung on to the back of the settee, her face colourless except for the hectic flush along her cheeks and her swollen, bruised lips.

'You wanted to talk to me. Is this it? Did you just want to insult me? If there's anything else, say it and go.'

'Oh, I've said it, lady,' he grated harshly. 'There's nothing else I could say to you!'

He walked out and the slam of the door was exactly what she expected. Didn't Kane always slam doors? She locked up tightly and then began to weep away the new shock and the longing that was now worse than ever.

She spent the rest of the night simply walking about, drinking endless cups of tea, and morning brought the realisation that she could no longer stay in Oxford. While Kane was here she was not safe. One more time like last night and she would forget everything but her longing to be in his arms. She would tell him the truth and she would be at his mercy.

There was a week free. She would go home. If that was not enough then she would simply stay there. No qualification was worth the amount of misery she was suffering at the thought of meeting Kane again. She packed a small case, ate a dry piece of toast when the idea of anything on it threatened to make her sick, and as soon as it was light she left the flat.

Her car was standing outside, the little Citroen 2CV that Kip had bought her. It was green and white, gaudy according to John and quite unmistakable. Nobody else here had a car exactly like it. The fact had always amused her. It did nothing to bring a smile to her face today, though, and she threw her case on the back seat, walking round to unlock the door and drive off.

She saw the Jaguar then, but it was not its sleek lines that held her wide-eyed gaze. It was coming towards her and the driver's eyes were intent on her face.

It was Kane, still looking as he had done last night, his shirt without a tie, his jacket nowhere to be seen.

'Andrea! Wait!'

He leaned out to call to her and then accelerated, and panic hit her in a wild wave. She couldn't face him again, hear his apologies, look into his eyes; she would beg to go with him—she was almost ready to beg now. She almost fell into her car, starting up at once and driving off before he could even begin to turn. The roads were clear and she drove recklessly, her only thought to lose him—and she even imagined she had done that.

When she looked into the driving mirror, though, he had turned and was coming up fast, the speed of the car he drove making her own efforts puny.

'No! No!' She began to mutter to herself, her foot hard down on the accelerator, her breathing fast and uneven, not one of her thoughts really on the road.

She was taking the corner too fast. Deep inside, her mind acknowledged this fact and reassured her that there was as yet nobody about. Her mind, though, was not capable of controlling the wheel nor the speed as she turned the corner. The little car went on to two wheels, the tyres screaming, and Andrea screamed too as the front bumper caught the wall and flipped the car like a toy, turning it over into the deep ditch at the side of the road.

Blackness had enveloped her long before then and she didn't see Kane leap down beside the car, his hands tearing at the door, his strength forcing open the crushed metal. He reached for her, her name a desperate whisper on his lips as he gently lifted her free and cradled her in his arms.

It was a long time before she was fully aware of her surroundings and even then the pain in her head was too bad to allow any movement. She was in hospital, she knew that. The walls were white and stark, the lights too bright. Inside her head, darkness came and went as she struggled to hang on to consciousness. She closed her eyes again but opened them almost at once as warm, strong fingers covered her own.

'Kane.' Her lips formed his name but no sound came. She knew his touch. It calmed her fears. She couldn't see him beside her as she moved her eyes but he seemed to realise that she must not move her head because he shifted his position, moving the hard chair into her line of vision.

'Oh, Andrea! Why did you do it? Why?'

His voice was almost as haggard as his face. He was white beneath the golden tan, his eyes red-rimmed, his grip on her fingers tight. All she could think of was that he was still wearing the same things, the remnants of his evening dress: the black trousers, the white silk shirt. He needed a shave, she thought vaguely, and his hair was all tousled. How she loved him! She would never love anyone else.

'You haven't changed since last night,' she whispered in a faraway voice, and his fingers gripped even more tightly.

'Andrea!'

The way he said her name, with a sort of hopeless desperation, made her eyes fill with tears. Her lips trembled.

'I'm hurt, Kane.' Her far-off murmur made him wince and his face looked even more drawn than before.

'It's concussion. I know your head hurts but you'll be all right. Just keep still. Everything's going to be fine.'

'Is it?' A tear trickled slowly down her cheek, followed by another one. Nothing was going to be all right. She wanted Kane to lift her up, take her away, hide with her, never let her go. 'Kane!' Her voice choked and he murmured her name softly.

'Shh! You're safe.' His fingers captured the tear, wiping it away and foolishly she remembered his words when he had caught her tears hungrily in his mouth, telling her he even wanted to possess her tears.

'Kane.' Her whispered words broke on his name and it seemed to be more than he could bear. He stood and leaned over her.

'I can't touch you, Andrea. I'm not allowed to. You have to rest. Don't cry,' he begged huskily.

For a moment their eyes met, clung, spoke and her pale cheeks were tinged with colour at what that tawny gaze told her. For a moment she didn't even feel pain. Their eyes locked together, exchanging vows. It was unforgivable, unthinkable, but they both knew the meaning of the message that flashed between them and the hard mouth relaxed from bitterness and smiled, his face softened.

'Darling.' Kane's voice was huskily gentle and his fingers slowly touched her face, tracing it gently.

'Get out of here! Keep away from her!'

They had not heard the door open and John's voice, so unlike what it was at any other time, was choked with rage, his eyes blazing with anger as he stood and looked at Kane.

'It's your fault that she's here! It's your fault that she's been slowly fading away! Haven't you done enough harm already? Get out of here, you bastard!'

'John!' Andrea tried to raise her head and groaned with pain, sinking back drawn and white to her pillows.

'Don't move!' Kane ordered urgently and, almost as if her body was attuned to his command, she relaxed. It wasn't lost on John.

'I phoned Kip,' he announced, his voice wild with anger. 'Luckily he was already on his way down here because they must have let him know. As a relative he can order you out but I'm not waiting that long. You get out of here now or I throw you out.'

'You can try,' Kane said in a deceptively soft voice. 'The only way I'll leave here is if *she* tells me to go.'

Bells seemed to be ringing in Andrea's head. Bells of joy because of the message of his eyes. She could still hear his husky endearment, still feel the tender touch of his fingers against her cheek. But it altered nothing. It was still unthinkable, unforgivable. He was married.

He loved her. His eyes had told her that and she believed those eyes, trusted them, but with that one look they had both betrayed his wife. Her heart was almost giddy with happiness but it was a happiness that would have to last a very long time—forever.

'Andrea?' John's voice was still trembling with rage. 'Tell him he's not wanted here. Tell him to go.'

She closed her eyes, her hands limp on the white sheets.

'Please go, Kane,' she whispered.

For a second he stood perfectly still and then his fingers stroked gently down her cheek before he walked quietly to the door and out into the corridor.

Andrea lay quite still, not wanting to speak at all, her pain nothing to her although it was severe. The pain in her heart was healing. Kane loved her. He loved her.

'Andrea?' When John spoke quietly she wanted to tell him to stop, to leave her. For a few moments she must savour the look in Kane's eyes because it was all she would ever have.

Her wish was granted because the sister came in and ordered John out too, her voice kind but very firm indeed, and Andrea made no protest at the pain-killing injection. When she woke up, she would remember. As she slid out of pain and into darkness she was smiling, her lips forming the huskily spoken word. 'Darling.'

For many days she knew little of her surroundings. The clarity with which she had known of Kane's presence seemed to fade. She knew that Kip came, that he sat beside her for hours on end, that he murmured to her reassuringly, telling her that everything was all right. She knew that Kane did not come back.

John came sometimes, his voice back to the quiet voice she knew so well. There·was something he was sorry about but she couldn't quite grasp what it was. The only voice that seemed to linger in her mind and penetrate the pain was Kane's, the one word he had spoken to her like a beacon of light through her dark days.

'He loves me,' she told Kip once when she was almost fully awake, and she knew he understood as Kip always understood her.

'I know. Get well, love. It's all right.'

Poor Kip. He would use any trick to bring her back to the world of the living. It made her smile and she slept more easily after that, the smile lingering on her face, making the sister beam at Kip when she came into the room.

'I think she's on her way,' she said with deep satisfaction.

'Thank God for that!' Kip ran his hand wearily over his face, noticing for the first time that he seemed to have started growing a beard. It intrigued him and sister laughed softly.

'You can leave her now. You need to sleep yourself. Tomorrow she's going to want someone to talk to, unless I'm mistaken.'

Andrea opened her eyes to sunlight and closed them rapidly. She seemed to have been in darkness for so long that the brilliant light almost hurt.

'I'll draw the curtains across. You can adjust to the light slowly.'

With the room darkened, Andrea could see that it was the same sister who had spoken. It was funny that she seemed so familiar when Andrea had not even seen her clearly before. She remembered snatches of conversation, though. It was the voice that was familiar.

'How long have I been here?'

'Eight days exactly. Do you remember your accident?'

'Oh, yes.' Andrea shuddered and then looked puzzled. 'I can't feel any pain. Did I break something?'

'Not exactly. You've had very severe concussion. For most of the time you've been merely on the edge of consciousness. Head injuries are tricky and I suppose we could say that you've had a lucky escape. Even so, you need plenty of rest now and a great deal of quiet.'

Kip told her the same thing when he came in later. By that time she had noticed that her room seemed to be filled with flowers. Everyone who knew her had sent large bouquets but she knew that Kane would not have done so. He couldn't, no matter how he felt.

His voice still lingered in her head, the promise of his eyes glowing in her mind. They had no right to love each other but they did. It would last forever.

'I've forbidden any visitors,' Kip said quietly, his eyes on her face. 'Don't expect John, or—anyone.'

'I don't.' She looked at her brother and smiled. 'You can stop worrying, Kip. Nobody can hurt me. I'm going to be a happy old maid. Kane loves me.'

'You told me.' Kip looked at her steadily. 'It was the only clear thing you've said for days. When you're able to leave here, I'm taking you home where I can watch you like a hawk.'

'I'm staying in Oxford,' Andrea said firmly.

'Kane's gone.' Kip eyed her warily but her smile defeated him.

'I know. He had to, don't you see? It makes no difference. I'm staying here. As an old maid, I'll need my qualifications.'

'My crazy little sister.' He smiled and took her hand. 'You're coming home. You need rest and, in any case, you owe it to Aunt Maureen—and to me. All your—friends want you to get better.'

'How has Aunt Maureen taken it?' Andrea asked anxiously, her eyes on Kip's serious face. 'How did you know I was here?'

'She's taken it badly, and I knew you were here because I had a phone call. I came straight away.'

'Of course, the hospital——'

'No. They didn't get the chance. Kane phoned me. He got you out of the car and into hospital. While you were being X-rayed. He phoned me and had me flown down. He stayed with you until you threw him out.'

'I—I had to send him away, Kip. He surely knew that?'

Tears glazed her eyes and Kip took her hand in a firm grip. 'Don't, sweetie,' he murmured with an anxious look at her. 'Of course he knew. He wants you to get well too. Come home.'

CHAPTER TEN

ANDREA finished clearing up her flat and settled down with a well-earned cup of tea. She had returned to Oxford the previous evening after three weeks at home, her aunt's well-meaning solicitude finally threatening to stifle her. In any case, she was better; her check-up that morning at the hospital had confirmed that. Now her flat was cleaned and polished and she was ready to get back to work.

Everyone had been almost too kind. Even now there were fresh flowers in the flat that had been delivered that morning from college and John had called round earlier, his old attitude back. He was just her friend again, and she was grateful for his understanding.

Neither of them had mentioned Kane. It was something they had both decided not to talk about without a word being said. John was still feeling guilty about his burst of rage and Andrea wanted to keep Kane to herself, securely in her heart. Even Kip had not mentioned him. She knew that Kip was fit again and that soon he would be going back to Africa, and she assumed that Kane was already there. He had told her he would go back—he had told her that a long time ago.

How would he and Kip react to each other now? It had been quite clear in the beginning that her brother was very attached to Kane. He had always acknowledged him as a friend. Would that friendship be ended because of her? She hoped not, and it was not a selfish thought. If Kane loved her half as much as she loved him, he would need friends.

She sighed and pushed the thought of him out of her mind. She would never see him again, not now, not when he had admitted with a look and a word that he loved her. He knew as she did that it was impossible and wrong but it was so little, the only thing they could share.

She had hardly begun her tea when the bell rang and she got up to answer it, knowing it would be John. He had promised to collect some books for her and they had arranged to have dinner together later on. She was smiling when she opened the door but her smile faded and her heart seemed to leap in her chest as she found Kane standing there, his eyes already on her face.

She just stood looking at him, only the fact that she held on to the door keeping her upright. He looked just the same, a tanned giant, his body more powerful-looking than ever in dark jeans and a casual shirt. She couldn't look away, couldn't speak, and it was Kane who finally spoke, his deep voice huskily soft.

'Do I get invited in?' His golden eyes mocked her and she flushed softly, backing away, mesmerised.

'Of—of course. How—how are you?'

'Very well, thank you, and you?'

'I—I'm fine now, thanks.'

He nodded seriously, stepping inside and closing the door, looking down at her. 'Well, that's got the polite preliminaries over. The next thing you do is offer me a cup of tea, isn't it?'

Andrea could only stammer at him. His smile seemed to be taunting her, but there was a fire at the back of his eyes that made her legs weaker still.

'I see you've been cleaning up. The whole place smells of polish.' He looked round, noticing the flowers, and his face darkened unexpectedly.

'I couldn't send you any.'

'I—I understood. I never expected...'

'Maybe you expect too little,' he murmured. He looked at her intently. 'I wanted to send you red roses, a mile high.'

'Kane, don't!' Her urgent plea had his expression softening miraculously, his hand gently tracing her face.

'I love you.' He said it simply, his eyes repeating the message, and she turned away desperately, her hands covering her face.

'I mustn't hear it! You mustn't say it. You have no right to say it, to look at me like that. I—I've planned my life down to the last detail.'

'Get your doctorate, marry Alford and settle down to teach at some university. I know the plan but you missed something out. You're mine.'

Andrea looked at him with shocked eyes. What was he suggesting? Did he want her to go with him now, to ignore his wife? She turned away, her hands clenched tightly at her side, fighting the desire to do anything he asked.

'I'm not going to marry John. I never was. I said that to—to...'

'To defend yourself,' he murmured. 'I know. I know *now*. If I'd known before it would have saved us both a lot of misery and you a lot of pain. I'll never leave you again. You belong to me.'

'You're *married*, Kane! How can I forget that?' Tears threatened to well up but she fought them down. She had his love. It was all she asked. She didn't even have the right to that but she clutched it greedily, hugged it to her.

'I'm not married, Andrea, not now,' he said softly. 'Babs and I agreed to a divorce. It became final the week before I came to Oxford. When I came here with Adele I came to get you. I've come to get you now.'

She stared at him with pain-filled eyes, her face a small tragedy.

'You divorced her? Because of me?' Her voice was little more than a whisper and Kane watched her closely. He nodded and the tears came then, glistening in her eyes, trickling down her soft cheeks.

'Kane. Oh, Kane! How can we live with that between us? How can I be happy knowing that because of me——'

He didn't let her get any further. He stepped close and simply lifted her into his arms, rocking her against his powerful chest and looking down at her gently.

'No more. No more, baby,' he said softly, his Canadian accent suddenly very strong. 'Telling you the way I planned is not the sweet agony I imagined. I can't see you hurt for even one second more. I've got a lot of explaining to do and you're going to listen, because I'm not about to stand back and see you cry.'

She was beyond protesting as he walked to the settee and sat down, settling her on his lap. He cuddled her against him, his hand pulling her silken head to his shoulder.

'Now I'm going to talk and you're going to sit still and listen.' He tilted her face and looked down into her eyes. 'No tears,' he murmured, his eyes skimming over her face, 'And don't look at me like that. I promised myself I wouldn't touch you until you knew the whole story. I've already broken that promise but I'm definitely not going to kiss you. If I do, there'll be no story at all.'

He pulled her back to his shoulder and in spite of everything she found herself relaxing against him, the tension that had been inside her for months easing away at his touch. Only the spectre of his wife held off her

happiness, and she waited with a sort of dread for Kane
to speak.

'Babs and I were married when we were twenty-one,'
he began carefully. 'I'd known her all my life and we
were fond of each other. Her name was Barbara Carter.
She was the granddaughter of the other half of my
father's firm. I suppose the affection we had for each
other and the pressure we were under to join the two
halves together made marriage inevitable. Neither of us
had ever been in love and I just didn't believe in it
anyway. We were very sensible. We thought affection
would be enough. It wasn't. Our marriage was stale from
the beginning and we both resented it.

'I was away a lot ...' he shrugged wryly ' ...as often
as I could get away, I guess. When we were forced into
each other's company we bickered with increasing bitterness. It was hopeless and we both knew it. Finally we
sat down and faced facts. A bad marriage was ruining
a lifetime of friendship. We parted, went our separate
ways. That was twelve years ago, long before I met you.
Does that help?' he finished quietly, lifting her face to
read the truth in her dark eyes.

'Why didn't you tell me? Why didn't you explain?
I've been so unhappy.'

She looked up at him with soft reproach and his dark
brows bunched together for a second as he read the pain
in her eyes.

'You were almost as young as I had been when I made
a very big mistake and got married,' he explained quietly.
His hand stroked back the cloud of fair hair, his golden
eyes softened incredibly. 'Oh, Andrea, honey. You were
full of life and high ideals. You were flung into a situation of danger, adventure. We were alone together and
in spite of my knowledge of how wrong it was for you
I couldn't keep my hands off you. I loved you—wanted

you.' He crushed her against him, his face against her hair. 'Darling, I wanted to tell you, especially when you cried that night in Nairobi, but it was just an episode in your life, something that would never happen again. Babs and I had made a mistake and rectified it like two sensible adults. I didn't feel sensible about you. I couldn't bear the thought of another mistake because I would never have been able to live with it—not if it was you. It was better to let you go, give you time to see how you really felt. If you had belonged to me I could never have let you leave me.'

'I couldn't get over it.' Andrea's lips trembled and she bit them together. 'You never came back. It seemed like a lifetime.'

'For me too,' he whispered, looking down at her with glowing, passionate eyes. 'The law takes its time and there were complications. Babs was living happily with another man, a French Canadian. He was wanting to get married but she was still hanging on to the thought of not hurting me.' He gave a soft laugh. 'I bet two men have never been so glad to see each other before. It was all very amicable but the law then dragged its feet and I didn't want to come to you until I was really free.'

'You—you just sat and nodded politely at me,' Andrea. reminded him tearfully. 'I thought Adele was your wife. I don't know how I coped.'

'Nor me,' he muttered grimly. 'The first time I'd seen you in months and another man's arm was round you. I knew I'd been right all along. It was only the adventure, the excitement. Oh, Andrea, I thought you'd just forgotten me.'

'I couldn't! I loved you. I could only tell Kip.' She touched his face wonderingly, almost afraid he would disappear, and he turned her hand to his lips, no trace of the hard, powerful Kane Mallory in his gentle touch.

'And how was I supposed to know?' he asked softly. 'I followed you that night, do you know that? I rushed Adele home and then hung around waiting. When you came out I followed.' His hands tightened on her. 'He was kissing you. I saw you in the headlights.'

Andrea remembered then, remembered too how she had felt.

'I was so lonely, so lost that it didn't seem to matter. I knew I could never respond to anyone but you. When the headlights shone on us I suddenly felt guilty, as if I was betraying you. It was a strange feeling.'

'Because I was there; even though you didn't know it, your heart knew it,' Kane said softly. 'It's how we are, my darling. I would have known but I was so filled with jealousy and despair, so sure that you were reacting as I had feared. The next time I saw you you were pacing about waiting eagerly for John Alford to appear. The first thing he did was grab you as if he owned you. I wanted to snatch you away, pick you up, *make* you come with me!'

'Instead you were nasty to me,' she reminded him.

'Not as nasty as I was on the night of the ball,' he muttered grimly. 'I could see you almost falling apart in front of my eyes and I was so blinded by jealousy that I never even started to ask myself why. All I did was hurt you. I walked up and down outside your flat for hours that night. I thought that bizarre little car was *his*. When the light went out I couldn't stand it. In the end I hammered on the door with every intention of breaking his neck. All I did was hurt you more and you made it quite clear that you didn't want anything to do with me.'

'I thought you were married, Kane!' she said in a plaintive little voice.

'Shh!' He kissed away her tears, his lips lingering against her eyelids. 'We've really managed to hurt each other, my sweet Andrea. I hurt you most of all. When that car turned over I thought I'd lost you. When I discovered you were alive I think I prayed every minute all the way to the hospital.'

'Why did you come back that morning?' She wound her arms round his neck, looking up at him with wide, dark eyes, and his resolve slipped enough to have him talking between urgent kisses that he placed on her cheeks and her smooth forehead.

'I'd just been on the phone to Kip. I was so damned miserable that somebody had to hear about it. I got him out of bed.' He stopped kissing her and grinned at her wryly. 'I got the sharp edge of his tongue in the true Forsythe manner. He wanted to know what I'd done to you this time. He asked me why I thought you looked as if you were fading away. I said you were clearly overworked and he stopped even trying to be reasonable. He stared shouting at the top of his voice, nearly taking my ear off. After threatening to come down and spread my person all over Oxford, he yelled, "She loves you, you bloody fool!" He slammed the phone down and I shot off to get back to you.' He shuddered. 'I nearly killed you.'

Andrea clung to him tightly and then leaned back with a little frown, looking into his eyes.

'We tell lies, you and I. It's caused all this misery.'

'You tell lies,' he corrected huskily, his hands beginning to mould her softness. 'You had me convinced you were marrying Alford—your *friend*!' he finished, his caresses stopping as he looked down at her with stern tawny eyes.

'How did you find out?' She looked at him a bit anxiously, knowing his considerable temper, and he let her stew for just about one second before he grinned at her happily.

'Oh, quite a few little dramas were acted out while you lay in that hospital bed, lady,' he remarked drily. 'I left the room when you told me to go but I didn't leave the hospital. I could see the trouble that would have ensued if I had insisted on staying with you. I'd not had the chance to explain to you and I was scared stiff that any sort of commotion would kill you. You looked so pale, so hurt. I would have walked out of your life right then to get you better but I had already looked into those dark eyes. I didn't need Kip to tell me you loved me.'

'John got turned out too,' Andrea pointed out, and he nodded with satisfaction.

'He came straight across to take me apart.' Andrea's eyes widened, her imagination seeing what would have happened to John if he had even tried it, and Kane smiled smugly.

'Kip walked in right then. I'd had him flown down and he came in the nick of time and put a stop to any violence. You've got a pretty tough brother there, honey. He sorted it all out and John admitted that he already knew how you felt.'

'He told me he would step back for anyone I loved,' Andrea said, her smile reminiscent.

'He doesn't love you,' Kane said urgently.

'I know.' She looked up into the golden eyes and smiled. 'He's my friend, nothing more. We're not idiots, John and I.'

'Stop bracketing your names together,' Kane demanded hoarsely. 'You're mine.'

'I know that too,' she said softly. 'I've always known.'

He looked at her intently, his eyes examining every feature, his hand coming to trace her face, and she felt the old wave of fire, her legs weak, her hands trembling, her eyes locked with his, drowning in the golden blaze.

'Next week, we'll be married,' he said huskily, his eyes on her trembling lips. 'Once you said you would be any- thing—my mistress. Stay with me until we can be married, darling. I don't want to spend another minute without you. I'm scared as hell that if I turn my head away you'll be gone. Live with me until you're mine forever.'

Andrea was trembling uncontrollably, her body soft, boneless, and he caressed her softness with increasing urgency, his lips searching her skin, her closed eyes. His kisses grew fierce, demanding, his hand holding her head to his as his free hand urgently slipped the buttons of her blouse.

'Andrea! My soft, silky darling!' His voice was a gasp of pleasure as he rediscovered the enchantment of her breasts and Andrea responded ardently, murmuring his name, her fingers feverishly plucking at his shirt, desire making her heart race under his hand.

His hands left her willing body, spearing into her hair, cupping her face as the golden gaze robbed her of all sense of time and place. There was only Kane, his power melting her, his strength making her weak.

'We made our vows, we made them right there in that hospital when you lay and looked at me. Our eyes said all we'll ever need to know. You need loving. Sleep with me, darling.' His voice was thick, shaking, but he wasn't begging. It was a command and she wound her arms round his neck, her trembling body pressed close to his as he stood and moved to the bedroom.

They couldn't stop looking at each other as he put her gently on the bed. She was back in time as if there had been no separation, Kane's golden gaze holding hers as he gently undressed her.

'I remember every inch of you,' he whispered thickly. 'I've spent every minute of these past months longing for you, the taste of you on my lips as if you were there. Sometimes, it's been unbearable.'

Andrea knelt on the bed, her fingers shaking as she unfastened his shirt and when she came to the belt around his waist her courage almost deserted her. She bit into her lip, her mouth trembling, and Kane tilted her face, his eyes smiling at her.

'I belong to you,' he said softly. 'I've belonged to you since our eyes first met. Don't be shy, darling. You're my brave, sweet girl.'

His muscles clenched with passion, though, as she touched him, and in the end it was Kane who took control, his breathing uneven as he completed the task himself and took her in his arms, pushing her gently back against the cool sheets. For a few minutes they lay close, gazing into each other's eyes until the blaze of gold melted Andrea's limbs and she moved against him with a low murmur of sound, a soft plea that brought his arms tightly round her.

His knees were sweet fire, urgent and fierce, covering every inch of her face and neck before moving to her smooth shoulders and the tempting curve of her breasts. She was drowning in sensation, willingly letting it sweep her under in a passionate tide, crying out with urgency as Kane's lips captured the rosy tip of her breast.

'Enjoy it, my love,' he whispered against her. 'Every part of me belongs to you.'

She belonged to Kane too and her soft murmurs of sound told him so over and over again.

When his hand slid down to cover the mound of her desire she twisted against him, her cries wild as his fingers coaxed the tender moisture, her stomach clenching with yearning. Waves of unendurable pleasure moved over her, her mind threatening to spin away, but she opened her eyes in dazed wonder and saw his smiling face, the tawny eyes watching her and her fingers clutched his arm.

'No, Kane,' she begged frantically. 'I want to belong to you.'

'And I want to love you, to please you,' he said huskily, his eyes on her wild, flushed face. His coaxing fingers moved again and she gasped with pleasure, shaking her head frantically.

'Let me belong to you!'

His lips stroked hers until they were breathing the same breath.

'And if I hurt you, my delicate little sweet?' he whispered into her mouth.

She looked up into his eyes and saw torment, desire and love. He was afraid of causing her more hurt and suddenly she felt as strong as Kane. She clung to him, her legs wrapping around him, tempting him beyond reason.

'I don't just want to belong to you in my mind, Kane. I want to be part of you. I want to know that you're inside me.'

'Andrea!' His hoarse cry was uttered against her parted lips and his mouth claimed hers urgently, open and demanding. For vibrant seconds they moved together with passionate compulsion and then Andrea gasped in pleasure and pain at the thrust of Kane's possession. Her own arousal accepted the fierce, powerful male body that claimed her own, her skin hot and damp, her mind reeling from the glory of it as they became lost in each other.

They soared out of the world, her cries of passion lost beneath the fierce pressure of his lips and when the world righted itself long minutes later she gazed in shy wonder at the man who held her tightly in his arms.

'Oh, Andrea,' he sighed on a shaken breath. 'I thought you'd never belong to me.' His hand stroked the damp tendrils of silver from her forehead. 'I seem to have done nothing but panic about your safety since I first met you. You're a small bundle of trouble.'

He smiled down at her and then eased his weight from her but she clutched him to her again, wide-eyed and pleading.

'Don't leave me, not even for a minute. I think I'll die if you do.'

'Shh, darling,' he whispered, kissing away her sudden and foolish tears as he gently withdrew. 'Leaving you gives me the exquisite joy of coming back to you. I'm going to spend the rest of my life proving to you how much I need you.'

He moved to his side and folded her against him, his hands stroking her skin. 'Love, love, love,' he murmured softly. 'I never knew there was such a thing, never knew I could feel what I feel for you. I could turn the world completely around if you asked me.' He sighed and tightened her to him. 'To think I might never have met you, never known that somewhere you were smiling and walking, living in a world that I knew nothing of. I believe in miracles.'

'So do I,' Andrea confessed shakily. Her body still trembled, still felt the vibrance of his possession, and her mind slowly began to accept that her hurting was over. It was like a wild, leaping joy, a miracle as Kane had said.

'I love you.' She eased herself up and looked down at him and his hand lifted to stroke her hair, his eyes smiling into hers. 'When I said it before, you didn't believe it.'

'Oh, I believe it now,' he murmured seductively, his eyes softened and he took her hand, raising it to his lips. 'You didn't have to prove it, my sweet girl. I just wanted to please you but you're altogether too much to resist, especially when you beg to belong to me.'

He pulled her down to him and for long minutes their lips met and clung in the lazy aftermath of passion. A sudden thought had Andrea sitting up in horror.

'John's coming!' she wailed, her cheeks flushed. 'We were supposed to be going out to dinner.'

'Wrong again,' Kane informed her, laughing up at her horrified expression. 'He knew I was coming back today. We met in the street and exchanged the usual pleasantries. He'll bring your books round tomorrow— if I let him in,' he finished with a frown. 'What you need from John is distance!'

'It seems to me that a whole lot of things have been going on behind my back!' Andrea knelt up and frowned down at Kane's satisfied smirk. 'For example,' she insisted, 'I'd like to know where you've been all these weeks!'

'Ouch! The nagging wife and we're not even at the altar yet.' Kane's strong hands gripped her waist, his expression changing subtly as his eyes roamed over the proud beauty of her breasts. 'I've been keeping away,' he murmured vaguely. 'Kip's orders and my own common sense.'

'Kane! Pay attention!' She tried to move but his hands only tightened and he smiled lazily.

'Oh, I am, I am.' He relented as her face flushed shyly and his smile was warm and loving as he looked into her eyes. 'We all wanted you to recover, darling, and I know what you can do to me. I agreed to keep clear until you were better. I knew that once we were together the inevitable would happen because neither of us can help it. Kip agreed not to tell you anything because I had to tell you myself. Your friend John agreed to behave very well.' He sighed. 'Where have I been? I've been back in Madembi, setting things up again, missing you and phoning Kip every day for news of you. All is serenity in Madembi now and the dam project gets underway next week, after the wedding—*our* wedding!'

Andrea's face clouded and she lowered her eyes to hide the sudden pain.

'You're going back there after—after we're married?'

'No. I couldn't leave you if I tried and I'm not about to try,' he promised softly. 'After the wedding, we go to Canada. If you want to finish here then I'll simply wait here for you. As for the dam, Kip takes over. He's about the best I've got and after the way he laid into me I've no doubt whatever that he'll keep everyone under tight control.' He reached out and tilted her face, forcing her to look at him. 'You don't mind? You'll not be worried about him?'

Andrea shook her fair head and smiled.

'I'm his sister, not his keeper. It's something he loves doing. It's where he wants to be.'

'And where do you want to be?' Kane asked gently, his tawny eyes capturing hers and melting her soul.

'Only with you,' she whispered.

He reached for her, his eyes running possessively over her creamy skin, the silken beauty of her breasts. He pulled her slowly and tenderly down to him.

'My beautiful, moonlit girl,' he murmured against her parted lips. 'Come here.'

HARLEQUIN 🛡 PRESENTS®

A Year
DOWN UNDER

In 1993, Harlequin Presents celebrates the land down
under. In May, let us take you to Auckland, New Zealand,
in SECRET ADMIRER by Susan Napier,
Harlequin Presents #1554.

Scott Gregory is ready to make his move. He's realized
Grace is a novice at business *and* emotionally vulnerable—
a young widow struggling to save her late husband's
company. But Grace is a fighter. She's taking business
courses and she's determined not to forget Scott's
reputation as a womanizer. Even if it means adding
another battle to the war—a fight against her growing
attraction to the handsome New Zealander!

Share the adventure—and the romance—
of A Year Down Under!

Available this month in
A YEAR DOWN UNDER

·A DANGEROUS LOVER
by Lindsay Armstrong
Harlequin Presents #1546
Wherever Harlequin books are sold.

YDU-A

Following the success of WITH THIS RING and
TO HAVE AND TO HOLD, Harlequin brings you

JUST MARRIED

SANDRA CANFIELD
MURIEL JENSEN
ELISE TITLE
REBECCA WINTERS

just in time for the 1993 wedding season!

Written by four of Harlequin's most popular authors, this
four-story collection celebrates the joy, excitement and
adjustment that comes with being "just married."

You won't want to miss this spring tradition, whether
you're just married or not!

**AVAILABLE IN APRIL WHEREVER HARLEQUIN
BOOKS ARE SOLD**

JM93

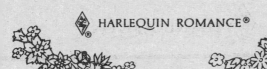

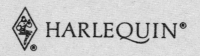 **HARLEQUIN®**

THE TAGGARTS OF TEXAS!

Harlequin's Ruth Jean Dale brings you
THE TAGGARTS OF TEXAS!

Those Taggart men—strong, sexy and hard to resist ...

You've met Jesse James Taggart in FIREWORKS!
Harlequin Romance #3205 (July 1992)

And Trey Smith—he's THE RED-BLOODED YANKEE!
Harlequin Temptation #413 (October 1992)

And the unforgettable Daniel Boone Taggart in SHOWDOWN!
Harlequin Romance #3242 (January 1993)

Now meet Boone Smith and the Taggarts who started it all—
in LEGEND!
Harlequin Historical #168 (April 1993)

Read all the Taggart romances!
Meet all the Taggart men!

Available wherever Harlequin Books are sold.

HARLEQUIN SUPERROMANCE®

HARLEQUIN SUPERROMANCE NOVELS WANTS TO INTRODUCE YOU TO A DARING NEW CONCEPT IN ROMANCE...

WOMEN WHO DARE!
Bright, bold, beautiful...
Brave and caring, strong and passionate...
They're women who know their own minds
and will dare anything...
for love!

One title per month in 1993, written by popular Superromance
authors, will highlight our special heroines as they face unusual,
challenging and sometimes dangerous situations.

Next month, time and love collide in:
#549 PARADOX by Lynn Erickson
Available in May wherever Harlequin Superromance novels are sold.

Where do you find hot Texas nights, smooth Texas charm and dangerously sexy cowboys?

AMARILLO BY MORNING

Show time—Texas style!

Everybody loves a cowboy, and Cal McKinney is one of the best. So when designer Serena Davis approaches this handsome rodeo star, the last thing Cal expects is a business proposition!

CRYSTAL CREEK reverberates with the exciting rhythm of Texas. Each story features the rugged individuals who live and love in the Lone Star State. And each one ends with the same invitation...

Y'ALL COME BACK...REAL SOON!

Don't miss *AMARILLO BY MORNING* by Bethany Campbell. Available in May wherever Harlequin books are sold.
